Riley

And The Secret Tunnels

To: Johnny, Jasmine, Legend + Nixon

Always follow your
dreams + keep reading!

BOOKS IN THE
RILEY CARSON SERIES:

Riley Carson
And The Secret Tunnels

BY
MEGAN WARGULA

Cover Design by
Megan Wargula & Andy Suggs

A portion of this book's profits will be donated to animal welfare organizations.

Ordering Information:
Quantity sales. Special discounts are available on quantity purchases by corporations, associations, and others. For details, contact the publisher at the address above.
Edited by Amanda Schuyler

Printed in the United States of America

Publisher's Cataloging-in-Publication data
Wargula, Megan.
Riley Carson And The Secret Tunnels / Megan Wargula
p. cm.
ISBN: 978-0-9973807-5-0
Library of Congress Control Number: TBD

First Edition

14 13 12 11 10 / 10 9 8 7 6 5 4 3 2 1

To Mom and Dad.

Thank you for your never-ending love and support. I am so grateful for the life you've given me. Your support of me means the world to me.

I love you.

Thank you for everything!

xoxo

"If a man aspires towards a righteous life, his first act of abstinence is from injury to animals."
-Albert Einstein

CONTENTS

A HEARTFELT MESSAGE TO MY READERS

I hope you enjoy book #3 in the Riley Carson Series! If you do like this book, it would mean so much to me if you would write a review on Amazon so more people can find my books and so we can change the world for dogs together! If you are under 13 or don't have an Amazon account, have your parent or guardian help you.

I love writing about Riley and her friends and it's because of you, the reader, that I am able to continue doing this. I always love hearing from my readers, so you can find me on social media, or send me a message through my website: RileyCarsonSeries.com. I look forward to hearing from you!

CHAPTER ONE

A Clue

Riley and Finn sat on the edge of their seats on Riley's front porch, looking at their friend Eve with excitement dancing in their eyes. "You think there's a clue to *treasure* in that book?" Riley asked as her eyebrows arched high over her blue eyes. Eve held a copy of *Gone With the Wind* in her hands and she thought it might contain some sort of clue!

As Eve flipped to the back of the thick tome given to her by their school librarian, Riley wondered if she could finish a book that long. "So, it's 719 pages long, and there are some blank pages at the end of the book. I flipped through them making sure there wasn't any more of the story left, or notes from the author. On what would be page 727, I thought I saw writing." Eve opened the book and turned to the second-to-last page. "I was reading it outside, it was really bright, and I swore I saw writing. The last page is thicker than all the rest, but I just knew something was there."

Riley and Finn looked at the book more closely as Eve demonstrated what she had found.

"These last two pages were stuck together, but I think it was on purpose," she explained. "I carefully peeled the top page off of the last page, and in small, faint handwriting, there's some sort of riddle!" Eve's dark eyes lit with excitement as she handed the book to her friends to see for themselves.

Riley read aloud, her words elevating with excitement as she read, "*You seek a place where treasure is found. Adventure awaits beneath the ground. Behind my back, there lies a clue. If you can read, you'll know what to do.*" Riley and Finn looked at Eve. Now all their eyes danced with excitement.

"This is so cool!" Finn looked closely at the words, tracing his index finger over them.

"Oh my gosh, this is awesome!" Riley agreed. "Did you find anything else?"

"No, there was nothing else on any page of the book, and I inspected it pretty closely after I found this."

Riley had a thought and asked, "When Mrs. Willnow gave you the book, it didn't have a dust jacket on it, did it?"

Riley could tell Eve had the same thought. "No, it came just like this," she pointed to the cornflower blue hardcover. "I wonder if there was another clue on the dust jacket?"

"Exactly what I was thinking," Riley said. "Behind my back there lies a clue...I wonder if it was on the dust jacket, and who knows where that is now. Probably long gone in the trash."

Finn was looking over every inch of the book now, determined to find something when Eve said, "I looked everywhere. There's absolutely nothing on or in the back of the book."

Finn had a gleam in his eye. "What if we carefully peel up this back page that's glued to the cover?"

"It's worth a try," Riley said, then looked at Eve. "Do you think that would be okay?"

Eve nodded, "When Mrs. Willnow lent me this book after we helped her catalog her purchase from the estate sale, she said that I could keep it because it was in rough shape and wouldn't be able to go in the system in the school library."

"That's right," Riley said. "This book probably came from the Powell's estate sale with the journal!" She held her hand out and looked at Finn. "Let me see." After Finn handed her the book, Riley looked it over noticing the cracking edges and yellowed pages. The book had that smell - the smell that only an old book had - not quite musty, just like old paper. "I think if we're careful, it would be okay. I mean, after all, she said you could keep it."

Eve nodded. "Yeah, and we'll want to be careful anyway in case the clue is under that last page. We want to keep it intact if it's there."

Finn agreed. "It's so old, I bet the back page will come up easier than we think. The glue is probably really dried out. You know I'm game to try it!"

The girls smiled, and Riley said, "We have to try. This could be the start of a new adventure!"

CHAPTER TWO

Upon Further Inspection

Once inside Riley's house, they were greeted by Buster, the family's rescued Yorkie. Finn and Eve squatted down to give him pets and scratches, then Riley scooped him up. "Let's go to the basement. All my craft stuff is down there."

Once in the basement, Buster settled under the coffee table as Eve set the book on top of it, and Riley grabbed her supplies. Finn was examining the book closely. He held the book by the front and back cover and tilted it forward, shaking out the pages. He looked at Eve and smiled. "Just in case."

Eve returned his smile. "I tried that. Believe me, I checked this thing out so closely once I found that clue."

"Let's just see if we can peel this page up first." Finn tried to get his fingernail under the paper, but quickly realized he couldn't. He held the book out to his friends. "Do either of you have nails long enough to get the corner up?" Riley showed her hands to her friends and shrugged. "Sorry, I can't stand long fingernails." She looked at Eve who was way more girly than she was and said, "Do you mind?"

Eve smiled and took the book. "Of course not." Ever so carefully, she peeled up the bottom corner of the page, but as she tried to peel it back further, it started to tear. "Shoot, this glue is pretty good."

"Oh no!" Finn said. "We have to be careful so we don't destroy the clue."

"Hang on," Riley said as she dug through her supply bin and pulled out a thin craft blade. "Let me see if I can get it with this." She pulled the safety cap off and worked the blade under the corner that Eve had exposed. Slowly, the paper was coming off the back cover. "The glue seems thicker around the edges," Riley said as she carefully worked with the blade. "I'm going to get the edges first, then hopefully the rest will peel off easier."

As Riley worked silently, Finn and Eve watched and waited. "This is so cool," Finn said. "I wonder where the next clue will take us!"

Just as he said this, they heard the paper tear. "Shoot!" Riley said.

"Be careful!" Finn warned.

"I know, I'm being careful. I think I just need to work slower," Riley said as she bit her lower lip and worked more slowly at the old paper.

Eve was smiling. As Riley seemed to work without another issue, Eve went back to Finn's comment. "I know, I couldn't believe it when I saw that clue. I'm glad I was finishing the book outside in the bright sunlight. The writing is so faint."

"I'm almost there," Riley said as she worked the bottom edge of the paper. Once finished, she sat back, "Okay, let's try to carefully peel it back. If it sticks any, we should stop.

We don't want to destroy the next clue if it's here."

Eve had an idea. "If it sticks too much, we could use steam to try to loosen the glue."

"Good idea!" Finn said, then thought for a moment. "As long as the steam wouldn't ruin the clue."

Riley was anxious to get started and went ahead and started peeling the page. She started from the bottom corner and worked slowly. It felt like the page was moving easily and they heard little cracks as if the glue was dry and coming apart, but so far, no tears. Riley felt herself biting her bottom lip as she concentrated on the task at hand. "I'm only going to peel back the bottom, top, and outside edges. I'll leave the inside edge attached so at least it still has a cover. If there's a clue here, we can expose the entire back without fully detaching the cover."

"Good idea," Eve said. "This book might actually be worth something since it's so old. I'd hate to completely destroy it. I mean, I already feel bad taking it apart like this."

"It's pretty worn, I doubt it's worth much," Finn said matter-of-factly as he continued to watch Riley work. He was watching Riley intently. "It looks like it's working!" Finn could hardly contain himself when he saw that Riley was successfully separating the old page from the cover. Riley smiled. Her best friend loved mystery and adventure, just like she did.

Riley's heart started to beat faster as her own excitement grew. She had the page almost midway up, but so far, she couldn't see any sort of writing or clue. She continued to peel back the page.

Eve was watching closely. "You're doing a great job, Riley."

Riley was glad the page wasn't tearing, but still couldn't see any evidence of a clue. Maybe it's at the top of the page, she thought hopefully.

As if reading her mind, Finn leaned in closer and said, "So far, no clue though."

"I'm hoping it's at the very top," Riley said as she was nearing the top of the page. The friends were silent as Riley worked. All three of them hovered closely over the book. As she peeled the page away to reveal the hardcover, Riley sat back and finally released the breath she had been holding.

Finn looked at the book closely. He pulled out his key chain which had a small flashlight on it and held the flashlight at an angle, inspecting the page and back cover closely for any signs of writing. "I don't see a thing."

Eve's shoulders sank. "I thought for sure it would be there! I've been over and over this book, and when you suggested that might be where we'd find a clue, it made total sense."

Riley said the words from the clue over again. "Behind my back there lies a clue." She inspected the outside of the back of the book and there wasn't a thing there, either. "I bet it was on the dust jacket."

Eve nodded her head. "Me too. That's the only other thing that makes sense."

Finn thought for a moment, then picked up the book and turned it over in his hands, inspecting it more closely than he had before. He set the book back on the coffee table and said, "When the book is on a shelf, the back is facing forward, or to the left, and the front is facing backward, to the right." He set the book on its end as you would do when putting it on a shelf. "Maybe the back is the front and the front is the back?"

Riley and Eve got excited. "I see what you mean!" Eve said. "Let's try to peel back the front cover from the backing." As she said this, she grabbed the book and carefully used her nails to peel up a corner. When she had peeled up the top corner, she handed the book to Riley who then began the slow process of removing the old paper from the hardcover in the front of the book. This time Riley worked from the top down, pulling the top, side, and bottom edges off cleanly. She was able to move a little more quickly this time and her friends were very quiet as she worked.

"Nope, no clue," Riley said as she sat back from the table. Buster took that moment to crawl into her lap and she lightly stroked him on top of his head.

Finn took his flashlight and examined the back of the page and the surface of the hardcover. "You're right. There's nothing here." He took a moment to fan through the pages, just to be sure.

Eve said, "I read every single page of this book and didn't notice any writing on any of the pages. I would have totally remembered when I saw the clue at the back." Riley could tell she was disappointed.

Riley rummaged through her bin and pulled out a glue stick. "Well, I guess we can glue this back together since we didn't find anything."

Eve nodded. "Yeah, go ahead."

Never to be discouraged, Finn said, "Well, I think our next stop is to go see Mrs. Powell to see if she happens to have the dust jacket. We can show her the clue and see if she thinks Mr. Powell wrote it. She may have some ideas as to where it's sending us."

"Good idea," Riley said as she finished gluing the pages back to the cover. "Besides, it's always good to see Mrs. Powell!"

CHAPTER THREE

The Downtown Pooch

The next day, Riley and Finn walked down Canton Street with Buster and Finn's rescued German Shepherd, Molly. Mrs. Powell would be home from church soon and told them she would be happy to see them. "We're meeting Eve at The Downtown Pooch, right?" Finn said as they neared their favorite pet boutique for supplies and food.

"Yeah, I told her I wanted to get the dogs some doggie ice cream on the way over so they could have a nice treat while we're with Mrs. Powell and Lily." Lily was Mrs. Powell's dog that Riley and Finn had found on their first day of middle school. Mrs. Powell adopted the sweet Maltese, and the kids were very fond of her.

Finn said to Molly, "Oh Molly, you're going to get a treat today!" Molly wagged her tail at the excitement and pitch of Finn's voice as they continued down the pretty, tree-lined street.

"I hope Mrs. Powell might have some ideas about that clue," Riley said as they strolled down the brick paved sidewalk.

"I know!" Finn said. "In that clue, 'beneath the ground' must mean tunnels. And we know there's a tunnel from the

Public House."

"And," Riley was excited now too, "it flat-out says treasure!"

"I know, I can't wait to see what she says!" Finn bounded up the steps that led to the front porch of the pretty white house where The Downtown Pooch was located.

"Hey guys!" Eve was sitting in an Adirondack chair on the front porch and got up when she saw her friends.

"Hey Eve," Riley said. "Thanks for meeting us here. I thought we should bring something for Lily. And by the time we get there, I think these two will be ready for some ice cream."

Buster and Molly were anxious to get in the front door, as were most dogs who walked by the friendly store. Riley knew the dogs could smell all the yummy goodness wafting out of the shop. She also knew how much the store's owner and the employees loved dogs, and lavished them with affection. Being a busy Sunday, both the owner, Sam, and her employee, Marina, were there, and as usual, they greeted the dogs with lots of pets and scratches.

"What can we get for you today?" Sam asked as she scratched Molly around her neck.

"A box of that peanut butter and bacon ice cream," Riley said. "We're going to take some to our friend's house, she has a dog too."

Marina finished petting Buster and said, "I'll go get it. It's back in the freezer."

As Sam rang up the purchase, she said, "You guys should be so proud of what you did for your neighbor."

Riley brightened at the thought of their neighbor Hawk and his pit-mix dog, Lennox. "Thanks, they are really special and I'm so glad we were able to help save Lennox from being put down. Now, we just have to get the city to repeal its ban on pit bulls."

Finn said, "Riley did all the work. Eve and I just helped where we could."

"Well, it's awesome, and I know how much it must mean to Hawk and his dog," Sam said as Marina came back with the ice cream.

As Riley handed Sam cash, Sam said, "I can't believe we have to deal with BSL in Roswell. There are so many awesome pit bull type dogs in this community, I just don't get it."

"We don't get it either," Eve said. "It doesn't make any sense to judge a dog based on its breed."

Breed-specific legislation was passed in Roswell, and it banned pit bulls and pit bull type dogs. Those who already lived in the city were grandfathered in, meaning they could still live in the city, but had to wear muzzles at all times when outside of their home or yard within the city limits.

"We're still working really hard to get it overturned," Finn said. "Riley even made this awesome design, and we're going to put it on shirts." Finn showed Sam and Marina a picture on his phone of Riley's "No Hate, Don't Discriminate" shirts featuring a smiling pit bull.

"When you have shirts, bring them here, and we'll sell them for you," Sam said. "And, if you want to set up a table to hand out information about ending BSL, you can have space on the lawn during Alive in Roswell."

Riley was so excited and appreciative. "Really? That would be awesome!"

"Yeah, we have a local shelter that sets up in the large area right out in front, but there's room for a table under the tree. We'd love to have you guys there. We need to educate as many people as possible so we can overturn that law."

"Thanks so much!" Finn said.

Riley was putting her money away and saw a poster on the front of the cash register area. "Oh, good, a found dog! Has she been reunited with her family?" The poster showed a picture of a yellow lab named Daisy who had been lost but now had been found. Riley always loved seeing those signs.

Marina said, "Yes, she was just recently found, and since we had lots of customers asking about her, we wanted to leave this up for a while so they would know we had a happy ending."

"How long was she missing?" Riley asked.

"A few weeks," Marina said. "It was just two days ago that she was found."

"That's awesome," Riley said. "At least they didn't have to miss her for as long as Baby Girl's family."

"You guys know Baby Girl?" Sam asked.

"Yeah," Finn said. "Riley and I spent a lot of time trying to find her. We thought we could help since we're always out riding our bikes and exploring, but we never saw her."

"Her family shops here," Marina said.

"No way!" Riley said. "We really did want to help find her. Do they think she was stolen?"

Riley noticed Sam and Marina exchange an uncomfortable yet knowing glance, but Sam said, "They really aren't sure. We don't think she was roaming around here because surely someone would have found her."

Marina pointed to two other posters on the front counter. "When you're out exploring, there are two more dogs that have gone missing. You should keep an eye out for them."

"Oh no," Riley said. She saw that some sort of smaller terrier mix was missing for a week, and a lab mix had been missing for a few days. "That makes me so sad."

"How did they go missing?" Finn asked.

"The smaller one got out of the house, just bolted apparently, and the lab mix got out of the yard. The family uses an electric fence, and apparently he just left the yard," Sam said.

Riley felt frustrated. "I hate those electric fences. Shocking a dog to keep it in a yard is so mean. Besides, if the dog wants to get out of the yard bad enough, it's one shock, and then he's good to go and can roam wherever he wants to."

"Seriously," Eve said. "Just get a real fence." Sam and Marina nodded in agreement.

The store had begun to get busy, so Riley snapped a picture of the Lost Dog signs and said their goodbyes. When they got on the porch, Finn said, "It's so sad about those lost dogs. We'll have to keep an eye out for them."

Eve agreed, then looked at Riley, her eyes alight with anticipation and said, "And Baby Girl's family shops here."

Riley felt her stomach turn. She had not only tried to find Baby Girl when she was lost, but she had also been wanting to locate her since she had been found. Riley thought the fact that Baby Girl had been gone for so long and was then found with some injuries needed further investigation. Riley wanted to touch the dog to see if she needed to communicate anything with her. When Riley and Finn first met Molly, she was able to communicate with Riley what she had been through. Riley couldn't explain it, but it had happened with Lily too. It didn't happen with all dogs, but when she touched certain dogs, Riley could see images of what they had been through. Unfortunately, it was usually when something bad had happened to them, and as uneasy as it made her, Riley knew she had to see if Baby Girl had anything to communicate with her.

CHAPTER FOUR

A Visit with Mrs. Powell

Riley, Finn, and Eve headed back down Canton Street toward Mimosa. Mrs. Powell should be home from church by now, and they were excited to ask her about the book and clue. When they arrived at her house, they saw Hawk's vehicle in her driveway. They walked up the wooden porch steps and as usual, Riley couldn't help but look up at the beautiful antebellum home with white columns. Finn knocked on the door and they heard Lily's barks.

Mrs. Powell opened the door, and her eyes sparkled. "Hi kids. I'm so happy to see you and the dogs!" Lily sniffed Molly and then Buster. She must have been happy to see them because she barked once and spun in a circle all while wagging her tail. "Mr. Hawkins is here too, with Lennox!"

"Oh awesome!" Riley said as she entered the large foyer. She looked to her left and saw Hawk in a chair with Lennox at his feet. Molly and Buster got excited when they saw Lennox and pulled on their leashes toward him.

"Hey guys," Hawk said. He looked at Lennox and gave him a command that let Lennox know he could get up and greet his friends.

Eve wasn't as used to being around all the dogs at once

and seemed to marvel at how well they got along. "They're all so well-behaved!"

It was as if the dogs knew not to be rambunctious in this pretty old home. They sniffed each other with tails wagging. Riley said, "This will help keep them occupied too." She opened the white bag with black paw prints all over it. "We bought doggie ice cream from The Downtown Pooch, and I'm glad I got the whole box because there are four in here. Is it okay for Lily and Lennox to have one?"

"Of course," Mrs. Powell said as she looked at Hawk who nodded.

"I'm sure Lennox will love it," Hawk said.

"It's bacon and peanut butter flavored," Finn said, then added, "But it's super-healthy."

"Then there's no doubt he'll love it!" Hawk said.

"Is it okay if I give it to them in here?" Riley said, still standing in the foyer.

"Absolutely, dear," Mrs. Powell said. "They aren't going to hurt anything. And I bet they won't waste a drop!"

Riley and Finn set the small ice cream cups on the ground, and the dogs tasted them. Lily seemed unsure of the icy treat at first, but then she must have enjoyed the taste because she started lapping up the soft ice cream. "It thawed a little on our way here, so that'll make it easier for them to eat," Riley said.

"Come, sit down," Mrs. Powell said. "We'll keep an eye on them from here."

The three kids sat on the settee across from the adults who were seated in a pair of chairs with wooden arms which had pale blue upholstery where your arms would rest. Eve pulled *Gone with the Wind* out of her backpack and handed it to Mrs. Powell. "We think this book might have come from your estate sale. Our librarian, Mrs. Willnow, gave it to me to read. When I got to the end, I could see faint writing on the back page and realized two pages were stuck together with writing on the very last page."

"It looks like the handwriting from the journals," Finn said. "Mr. Powell's journals."

Mrs. Powell examined the book and flipped to the very back. She got to the pages that Eve described, and she smiled as she ran her fingertips across the page. She tilted her head as she said, "Yes, this is James' handwriting. Oh, how he loved mysteries!"

"Do you know what the clue means?" Riley asked. Mrs. Powell read it aloud as Hawk contemplated it.

Finn said, "We thought it meant that the next clue was in the back of the book, but that's the last page, and there's no dust jacket."

Mrs. Powell inspected the book more closely now, doing much of the same things the kids had done. "I'm sure it came with a dust jacket, but that would be long gone, I'm afraid."

Hawk suggested, "Maybe there's something written on the piece that's glued down to the back cover?"

Riley shifted in her seat and hoped Mrs. Powell wouldn't be upset. "We tried that. We were able to carefully peel off the pages stuck to the back and front, but nothing was there." She added, "We were really careful and when we didn't find anything, we glued it right back."

Mrs. Powell smiled. "Oh, it's okay. I would have suggested that too! Now I'm curious about this." Mrs. Powell took the book and opened it right in the middle and peered down the binding. She smiled and said, "I wonder if there was something on the dust jacket..." She closed the book and handed it to Hawk.

Hawk flipped through the pages and looked at Eve. "Were there any markings on any of the pages? Was anything written anywhere in it?"

Eve shook her head. "Nope, and I read the whole thing. I didn't notice anything at all, and I would have."

Mrs. Powell looked at Eve. "Did you enjoy the book, dear?"

"Yes, ma'am," Eve said. "It really gave a glimpse of what life was like back then."

Riley shifted uncomfortably in her seat again, knowing what Eve's skin color would have meant for her back at a time like that.

Mrs. Powell smiled kindly and said, "Those were woeful days, indeed."

Eve said, "It's good that people like Margaret Mitchell wrote about those times, because it's hard for kids like us to even imagine what things were like back then. And I did love the characters so much. I want to know what ultimately happens to Scarlett and Rhett."

"I think that's why Margaret Mitchell wrote it the way she did, so you could form your own ending."

Riley liked that idea but didn't have much to add since

she had only seen the movie. She wanted to know Mrs. Powell's thoughts on the clue. "Mrs. Powell? The clue mentions treasure and underground. Is there anyone else in town who might know of a tunnel system?"

Mrs. Powell thought for a moment. "There might be a couple of people. Let me do some asking around, and I'll see what I can come up with for you."

CHAPTER FIVE

Checking with Mrs. Willnow

At school on Monday, Riley, Finn, and Eve went to see Mrs. Willnow during their lunch period. They had made friends with the librarian, and she was keen to help the kids with any of their school work or even their extracurricular activities. Mrs. Willnow was such a dog lover that she supported their work in helping dogs in Roswell. She had even adopted dogs that were rescued from a puppy mill. Riley just loved Mrs. Willnow!

As they entered the library, the kids scanned it for their favorite librarian. Mrs. Willnow had a small stack of books in her hands, shifted them into one arm, and waved at the kids.

Riley waved as a smile spread across her face. The three friends headed toward the shelves on the right where Mrs. Willnow was working.

"How are my three favorite students?" Mrs. Willnow asked with a wink.

"We're great!" Finn said. "In fact, we're hoping you might be able to help us with something."

"Uh-oh, I've heard this before." The kids had come to Mrs. Willnow when they were searching for the Cherokee Caves. She had no idea what their search for the caves would lead them to. No one could have imagined that. She looked at Eve. "What are you guys up to now?"

Eve smiled, "Nothing crazy. Remember that copy of *Gone with the Wind* that you lent me?" Mrs. Willnow nodded. "Well, we found what we think is a clue in the back, and we wondered if you remember the book having a paper dust jacket on it when you got it from the estate sale."

"A clue? What on earth does it say?"

Eve shouldered her backpack off her right shoulder and unzipped it. She pulled out the thick book and opened it to the page in the back with what they thought was a clue. Mrs. Willnow read aloud, *"You seek a place where treasure is found. Adventure awaits beneath the ground. Behind my back, there lies a clue. If you can read, you'll know what to do."* Mrs. Willnow looked up at three eager faces and said with excitement, "Well isn't that awesome?" She inspected the book just as the kids, Mrs. Powell, and Hawk had done.

Finn said, "We looked it over really well, we even peeled off the pages glued to the cover and took it to Mrs. Powell and Hawk, and they couldn't find anything either."

"We were hoping that for some strange reason it had the cover on it when you got it and just didn't end up with the book," Riley offered.

Mrs. Willnow closed the book and handed it back to Eve. "Nope, I'm afraid I got it just like this. Do you think there was another clue on the dust jacket?"

Riley nodded. "That's the only other thing we can think of since we didn't find anything."

Mrs. Willnow looked at Eve, "And you read the whole

thing? No markings on any of the pages?"

Eve nodded. "Yep, I read every page and there were no notes, markings, or anything out of the ordinary, and I would have noticed."

"What did Mrs. Powell say?" Mrs. Willnow asked.

"She said it was definitely her husband's handwriting and was sure it came with a dust jacket, but that she had no idea where that would be by now," Riley said.

"And, she said she knew of a couple of people who might be able to help with the clue, like if they've heard of any stories of buried treasure around here!" Finn said as excitement sparkled in his eyes.

Mrs. Willnow chuckled at this. "It's always adventure with you three!" Riley and Eve were smiling now, too. "I'm sorry I can't be of any help."

"It's okay," Riley said and offered a change in subject. "Hey, how are Maggie, Nikki, and Harley doing?"

At this, Mrs. Willnow's eyes lit up. "Oh, they are doing just great! Harley gets so much attention from the girls. Come here." She motioned for the kids to follow her back to her office where she pulled her cell phone out of a drawer. After tapping the screen a few times, she turned the phone toward the kids, and they saw the cutest picture of all three of Mrs. Willnow's rescue pups cuddled on the sofa, sleeping peacefully.

"That's so sweet!" Riley said as she moved closer to the phone. "Look how comfy they all are! I bet it feels like heaven compared to that awful puppy mill where they grew up." The picture showed Mrs. Willnow's two female Yorkies and male Chihuahua. Harley was the Chihuahua, and even though you couldn't really tell while he was sleeping, he was missing an eye.

Mrs. Willnow agreed. "It just boils my blood when I think about what they went through. Especially Harley."

Eve's voice was quiet when she said, "I still can't believe they would pressure wash a cage with dogs inside."

Riley shuddered at the thought of that disgusting place. "I still can't believe that puppy mills are legal."

"Me neither!" Mrs. Willnow said as she put her phone back in her desk drawer. "Dogs deserve so much better."

"Maybe we can change that," Riley said hopefully. "We just have to work hard to educate people about where dogs in pet stores or online breeders come from."

"I hope so too," Mrs. Willnow said then looked at Riley proudly. "You certainly did a great job helping your neighbor get his service dog back."

Riley felt content. "Yeah, I'm so glad we could help save Lennox. It really was a group effort." She looked at Finn and Eve who were smiling proudly.

Finn said, "Now, if we can just get BSL overturned!"

Mrs. Willnow nodded. "I'm happy to help in any way. I can't believe the city would be so foolish as to ban certain breeds of dogs. It just seems so archaic."

"I know," Riley agreed. "We don't judge people by the way they look, and the city is basically doing that when it comes to dogs. We're working hard to educate them that it's not the breed of dogs, it's how they are raised. Look at Lennox, he's a rescued pit mix who is trained to be a service dog. He's the sweetest, most loving dog. He wouldn't hurt a fly."

Finn said, "The Downtown Pooch is letting us set up in front of their store during Alive in Roswell. You should come by and see us!"

"I most certainly will! In fact, if you need help, just let me know, and I'll do whatever you ask," Mrs. Willnow said sincerely.

"If you can think of anything that might help us figure out this clue, let us know." Finn said as Riley caught a glimpse of something on their librarian's face that she couldn't quite place. "It would be so cool to find buried treasure!"

The bell rang signaling the end of their lunch period. "Okay, off you go. I'll let you know if I can think of anything." Just then Riley felt like Mrs. Willnow knew more than she let on. She had a knowing look in her eyes. But why wouldn't she say anything if she knew where the next clue was?

CHAPTER SIX

Alive in Roswell

The school year started to wind down, and Riley couldn't wait for summer break. While the end of the year meant exams and lots of studying, all of that would be over soon, and they would have time over the summer to work even harder to overturn the breed specific legislation that Roswell had passed. Riley hoped they could get through to the mayor and city council members. For now, she was excited to set up a table at Alive in Roswell so they could educate residents about breed specific legislation at tonight's event.

Riley and Finn arrived early with their parents. Their dads unloaded a table, chairs, and a box of supplies while their moms helped the kids arrange everything on the table so it was easy to see and uncluttered. They had clipboards with a petition, trifold brochures with all sorts of facts about why BSL didn't work, an email sign-up sheet, and stickers with Riley's "No Hate, Don't Discriminate" design. All of the volunteers would be wearing shirts with Riley's design, and many would be walking through the crowd to hand out brochures and stickers.

Riley stacked the stickers proudly at the front of the table. "That was so nice of the printer to print these for a discount."

Mrs. Murphy smiled. "It sure was. There are so many dog lovers in this town, including the owners of the print shop. It turns out that their son has a pit bull who they consider their grand-dog."

Riley smiled at that. "That's so great. It's amazing how many people have volunteered time and services to help us." As she was saying it, their friend Tim Harrington walked up. "Hey Tim!"

Tim wore his trademark flip-flops, one of his many University of Georgia t-shirts, and a pair of shorts. Riley felt like Tim belonged on a beach somewhere. He might be one of the most laid-back people she knew, and he was also very passionate about dogs. "Hey guys, what can I do to help?"

Finn sat behind the table and rummaged through a box. "Here's some chalk. Can you write on the sidewalk to let people know we're set up here?" Finn tossed the box of chalk to Tim.

As he caught it, Tim said, "What, you think I'm good at graffiti or something?" Everyone laughed because Tim had indeed gotten in trouble for tagging city hall with anti-BSL slogans, including Riley's design. He fortunately got off easy but was still doing community service.

"I've seen your work," Finn said. "You do have an artistic side."

Tim chuckled as he headed to the brick paved sidewalk and passed by Riley who tied balloons to the railings on either side of the stairs that led up to The Downtown Pooch. Riley saw two ladies heading toward her, passing out hand-held fans. "That's such a great idea!" Riley said as she nodded to the fans in the ladies' hands.

The brunette lady smiled and said, "Yeah, it gets hot out here, so it's a great way to advertise our business." She handed Riley several fans. "Here, take a few for your table."

"Thanks," Riley said. "Here are some stickers. We're trying to overturn the law banning pit bulls here." She pulled a stack of stickers out of her back pocket and gave each of the ladies one.

"Thank you," the blond lady said. "Do you have any literature we could put at our front desk in the office? We're big dog lovers."

"Of course." Riley grabbed a stack of trifolds from the table. "Here you go, thanks so much!"

"You're welcome. Stay cool tonight." The ladies headed down the street to pass out more fans.

Riley absent-mindedly fanned herself. It did feel good. She looked at the design on the fan. It said, "We're big fans of healthy spines!" It was for a chiropractic office with their contact info prominently displayed. Riley flipped it over and read, "We've got your back!" She had a moment of realization and pulled her phone out of her pocket. She called Eve. "Hey! Have you and Evan left yet?"

Eve replied, "We're just pulling out of the driveway."

"Wait! Can you bring the book? I think I have an idea where we can look to see if there's another clue." Finn walked up and looked at Riley quizzically.

"Sure thing," Eve said. "We'll see you soon!"

"What's up?" Finn asked.

Riley handed him a fan. "Check it out."

As Finn read the fan, then flipped it over, Riley saw his eyes light up with recognition. "The one place we didn't check!"

CHAPTER SEVEN

Confrontation with Corey

As Riley and Finn waited for Eve and her brother to arrive, they finished getting everything set up. More volunteers arrived after braving Atlanta traffic and Tim finished up his chalk work. A local rescue group had set up tents and a table in the large portion of the lawn across the walkway from them. Riley and Finn went to look at Tim's work. Tim had recreated Riley's graphic of a smiling pit bull with the phrase, "No Hate, Don't Discriminate" on the sidewalk. Instead of the cursive Riley had used on her design, Tim used a thick, blocky text and lots of colors and shadows.

"Looks great!" Riley said. "This will definitely attract attention."

"Yeah," Finn agreed, "The words almost look 3-D!" Finn said before his eyes fixed on something else. "Oh yay, look who's here."

Riley detected the sarcasm in Finn's voice and looked in the same direction. Down the block, Corey Thornton and his friends, Brad and Seth, headed their way. Corey was the class bully and picked on everyone, but he had zeroed in on Riley for some reason. He had become a thorn in her side. "Oh, joy," Riley said with equal sarcasm.

At that moment, Eve and Evan walked up behind them. "Hey guys," Eve said.

The kids turned around. "Hey!" Riley said and gave an eager smile. "Thanks so much for coming to help tonight."

"We wouldn't miss it," Eve said.

"What can I do to help?" Evan asked as he brushed his dark hair out of his left eye.

Riley looked at the table which was set up and sufficiently manned. "I think we're good for now." She checked her phone for the time. "We have about fifteen minutes until it officially starts." She looked across the lawn at the rescue group. A small, older lady wrestled with a large dog crate. "Since we're okay over here, maybe check with the rescue group to see if they could use your help?"

"Good idea," Evan said. His eyes brightened as he looked at the leashed dogs of various breeds and sizes. He headed over to see what he could do to help the mostly female volunteers who were wrangling several large dogs.

Eve opened her backpack. "Here's the book. What are you thinking we missed?" Riley held up the fan from the chiropractic office and showed Eve both sides, her eyes scanning as she read the fan. "The spine! How did we not think of that?" Eve asked.

Riley had the book in her left hand, cradling it against her waist when someone grabbed it out of her hand. Riley spun around to see Corey's chubby, ruddy face. "Corey, give it back!"

Corey smirked at Riley. "You guys really are nerds! Who brings a book to this event?"

Riley grabbed for the book, but Corey was too quick and lurched backward. He then tossed the book to Seth who lurked behind Corey. Now Finn rushed toward Seth, but he tossed the book back to Brad. Corey stepped up on the low stone wall that lined the sidewalk. "Give it here!" Brad tossed the book to Corey. He looked the book over and flipped the pages. "Did you really read this whole book? What a nerd."

Riley jumped up on the wall and headed toward Corey. "Why do you have to be such a pain?" Riley almost snatched the book from Corey, but again, he was quicker and moved it to his other hand. He prepared to launch it back to Seth when he suddenly heard loud, deep barking behind him. Riley swore she saw fear in Corey's eyes. Was Corey afraid of dogs? Startled, Corey's throw fell short of Seth, and the book landed with a crack on the ground.

Riley watched the whole thing play out as if in slow motion. Mrs. Powell's copy of *Gone with the Wind* had just cracked its spine on the sidewalk, and something fell out of the book. Tim scooped up the copy of the book as Riley hurried over and picked up what appeared to be a small piece of paper. She quickly tucked it in her pocket. Tim handed the book to Riley before facing Corey. He hopped up on the stone wall, practically getting in Corey's face. "What's your problem, Corey?"

Riley swore she saw Corey flinch. "Don't you have community service to do?" Corey said as he brushed past Tim and stepped down off the wall, joining Brad and Seth on the sidewalk. "Come on, let's go," he said to his friends as they followed behind him down the sidewalk.

"They are so annoying!" Riley said.

"I don't know what his deal is," Finn said. Then he switched to the more exciting matter. "Did I see something fall out of the book?"

Riley smiled, and the frustration with Corey and his friends quickly diminished. "Yes!" She looked at the book in her hand. The spine had a crease down the middle and the pages felt loose. She handed the book to Finn and reached into the pocket of her jeans. Riley pulled out a yellowed piece of paper that was folded several times. As she unfolded it, she saw hand writing they recognized as Mr. Powell's.

"What does it say?" Eve asked eagerly as she and Finn moved closer to see for themselves.

Sacred words are written within. While there are many versions, there is no twin. Our family tree runs very deep. If I lost this book, I would surely weep.

"Another clue!" Finn said with excitement.

Riley's mind was already turning, trying to figure out this clue when she heard Mrs. Murphy's voice. "Hey kids, are you ready to start manning the table?" Riley looked up to see Mrs. Murphy and her mom at the table with a large group of volunteers standing by.

Riley looked at her friends. "Any ideas?" They shook their heads. "Me neither. It looks like we'll have to spend some time with this clue too. Come on, let's go man the table so the adults can go pass out brochures and stickers in the street." Excited about the clue they found, Riley tucked it safely in her pocket. She knew she and her friends would rack their brains over it all night long.

###

Riley could feel the sweat on her back as the sun started to set behind the large tree across the street. Alive in Roswell was only halfway over, but they already talked to a lot of people. Several of the adult volunteers returned to get more stickers and brochures.

"I hope this means we're educating a lot of people," Riley said as she handed a large stack of brochures to a familiar volunteer.

"I think we are," Mrs. Willnow replied. "Don't lose faith. Together we can do great things." And with that, she was off to talk to more people. It made Riley's heart swell to know how many people cared about this issue and that Mrs. Willnow had come to support them on such short notice. Sometimes it can feel like you're the only one who cares, but there was a lot of support to repeal BSL in Roswell and for that, Riley was grateful.

Eve and Tim handed out flyers on the sidewalk before Eve returned to the table. "I'm going to see if they need any more brochures or stickers inside." She nodded to the front door. "It looks like they've been busy in there."

Riley got more brochures out of a box under the table. "Cool. Thanks, Eve!" Finn was reviewing the pages of the petition on his clipboard. "I've gotten a lot of signatures, close to one-hundred! If the other volunteers who are walking up and down Canton Street have this many, that'll be awesome!" Riley was about to say something when Eve ran up, her brown eyes dancing with excitement. "Guys! I think Baby Girl is inside!"

Riley's stomach flipped as she fidgeted with her key necklace. She looked at Finn for guidance. "You've gotta go meet her," Finn said. "Even if she doesn't have anything to communicate, you were so worried about her."

"Honestly, I hope she doesn't have anything to communicate with me." Riley swallowed hard and headed up the porch steps to see if she could meet Baby Girl. Finn followed right behind her.

CHAPTER EIGHT

Meeting Baby Girl

When Riley and Finn entered The Downtown Pooch, they saw a lot of people browsing and lining up to pay for their purchases. Sam, waved at Riley from behind the counter and said, "How's it going?"

Riley smiled at the petite blond woman with blue eyes and said, "It's really great. We're talking to a lot of people about BSL." There were customers at the register, so Riley was brief. She searched the dogs in the front of the store and so far, didn't see Baby Girl. The shop was in an old home, so it felt crowded even with a handful of people in one room. Off the front room was a narrow hallway that led to a room in the back that offered food and treats, then to the right held another room with toys and gifts for pet lovers. A small hallway at the back of that room led to smaller rooms, one with a large refrigerator, one with cat stuff, and a room she assumed must be an office. Riley liked to imagine how the building was set up when it was a house. It felt so small and closed off compared to modern homes. So far, Riley didn't see Baby Girl.

Finn searched too and said, "Well, maybe they've left already." He motioned to the back door that led to the parking lot.

Riley really wanted to meet Baby Girl since she had followed her case so closely but experienced a mix of emotions. She felt disappointed and relieved at the same time. Riley turned to head back toward the room with the food and treats. "Maybe they're in here," she said. "The shelves are so tall, they could be in the back of the room. As they waited for people to cross in front of them and head out the back door, Riley felt something brush up against her left leg.

"Baby Girl!" A woman's voice said. "Don't be rude."

Riley could feel her heart skip a beat as she and Finn turned around.

"I'm so sorry," a smiling lady with brown hair said. "She's usually not so forward with people. Quite the opposite, really."

Riley looked at the pretty, rust-colored dog who she had followed online for so many months. The dog was a medium-sized lab mix whose dark eyes seemed to sparkle as she gazed up at Riley. The pretty dog looked almost like she did in her pictures, but she appeared thinner and had small marks on her face. Riley swallowed hard and looked at Baby Girl's mom. "I've followed her online since she went missing. Finn and I searched for her whenever we were out riding our bikes or exploring Roswell." Finn nodded and smiled as she said this.

The lady smiled kindly. "Thank you so much. We were devastated when she went missing, and she was gone for so long. We were afraid we might never find her."

"We're so glad you did." Riley realized she hadn't introduced herself. "Oh, I'm Riley, and this is my friend, Finn." Riley gestured to Finn who stood just behind her in the small space.

"I'm Emily," the lady who Riley guessed was in her thirties said. "And, you know Baby Girl." She smiled as she looked down at her beloved dog, giving her a treat from a pouch on her hip. "Good girl."

"Is she okay if I pet her?" Riley felt her nerves flutter in her stomach. Before Emily could answer, Baby Girl raised her paw and scratched at Riley's leg.

"Baby Girl!" Emily said as Riley and Finn chuckled. "I'm sorry, she's never this forward around people."

"It's okay," Riley said. She squatted down to Baby Girl's level. "I'm a huge dog lover. She must sense that."

Finn said, "Yeah, Baby Girl probably knows she can trust Riley. I don't know anyone who loves dogs more than her."

Riley exhaled as she held out her hand so Baby Girl could smell it. Riley felt the little puffs of air as Baby Girl investigated her scent, then she gave Riley a tiny lick on her knuckles. "Hey, Baby Girl," she said sweetly. "You are such a good girl." Riley knew to approach an unknown dog, especially one known to be skittish, slowly and respectfully. Instead of reaching over the dog's head to pet her, she lightly scratched the dog on her chest, and after a moment, she started to "see" things. Finn's voice faded as he asked Emily questions about where they found Baby Girl. Riley tuned into what Baby Girl showed her. She heard muffled voices, likely men, but she couldn't make out what they said. Then she heard whining and barking. All at once, she felt sad, scared, nervous, and anxious. Her heart pounded in her chest. Powerful hands grabbed her neck and shoulders, and then a sensation of darkness came at her face. Sharp pain cut her face repeatedly and with force. It hurt, really badly. Loud, angry barking. A smell, the metallic scent of blood. All Riley wanted to do was run. Far away from wherever this was. Then, it all stopped. Riley felt her heart racing inside her chest then felt licking on her forearm. Joy and comfort washed over her, and she saw Baby Girl on a soft bed with a little boy. Now filled with peace and security. Riley's heart rate slowed down and she let out a breath she didn't know she was holding.

Riley knew she was starting to come out of her communication with Baby Girl. She didn't know what Finn and Emily might have seen on her face during this experience, but she knew she had to control her emotions and expression. Riley looked at Baby Girl who sat patiently as she continued to scratch her chest. Riley smiled at the sweet dog and talked to her. "I'm so lucky I got to meet you, Baby Girl. You are just the sweetest!" Baby Girl then rubbed her head against Riley's leg and sat right next to her. Riley took this moment to sit all the way down on the floor and now she scratched Baby Girl behind her ears. Riley and Baby Girl sat in between Emily and Finn. They were facing Finn because Riley still needed a moment to compose herself.

"Well," Emily said, "you must be a really big dog lover. I've never seen Baby Girl so comfortable with someone she doesn't know!" Her voice grew somber. "Especially since we got her back." Emily gave her dog another treat and a scratch on the top of her head. "You're being such a good girl," she said with a smile on her face and a praising sweetness to her voice.

Finn took a chance and asked, "Do you know what happened to her in the time she was gone?" Riley knew Finn tried stalling to give her time as she recovered from her experience by chatting with Emily.

Riley settled herself as she heard Emily inhale deeply, then exhale. "We aren't sure. She was very frightened. More skittish than she was before. She's a rescue and had been a skittish dog in general, but she was almost shell-shocked when we got her back. She used to be more leery of people she didn't know, but is now that way about other dogs too."

Finn said, "Well, it looks like she's getting better."

"We've been working with her a lot. In fact, a wonderful trainer who followed her story has helped us at no cost. Baby Girl has really improved so much. I wouldn't have brought her down here if she was as afraid as she was when we got her back. There's no way." Emily smiled down at Riley and Baby Girl who got another treat for being so good. "She never would have done this before. Riley, you must have the magic touch!"

Riley looked up at Finn, and he smiled knowingly at her. Hopefully, he could tell she started to feel better. "I told you. No one loves dogs as much as Riley Carson," Finn said.

Riley finally calmed since she felt those disturbing emotions from Baby Girl. She turned and smiled up at Emily. "I really do love dogs, so much! It's an honor to have a dog feel safe with you."

Emily smiled sweetly at Riley and nodded at Baby Girl who stuck to Riley's side like Velcro. "Well, you've certainly got a friend in Baby Girl...whether you like it or not."

All three of them laughed and Riley said, "I like it very much, don't I Baby Girl?" Her voice went up an octave as she spoke to the sweet dog who had clearly been through so much. Riley had to make sense of what she had just experienced. As soon as they said their goodbyes, she would need to write everything down. Every detail she saw and felt, and she knew that would be easy as she recapped it with Finn and Eve.

After they said goodbye to Emily and Baby Girl, Riley and Finn headed back through the front of the store and out the front door. Eve waited at the table which had so many volunteers, there wasn't enough room for them to help out. Riley called to Eve from the porch. "Eve, come up here."

Eve climbed the steps and the kids walked to the far end of the porch where they would have privacy. "So," Eve said, "did you get to meet Baby Girl?"

Riley's eyes widened as she looked at Finn and Eve. "I sure did, and she showed me a lot." Riley proceeded to recap what she had seen as Eve took notes for her on her phone. "It was really scary. I felt so much fear and...anxiety. Like I felt really stressed out. *Really* stressed out. I felt pain on my face, it hurt really badly. I felt like I wanted to run, I had to get out of there. It was dark and just oppressive. And there were dogs barking, just a lot of barking."

"Like at the puppy mill?" Finn asked.

Riley thought for a moment. "No, it felt different." She paused and tried to search her mind for what exactly was different about it. "The puppy mill sensation was like a depression, this was - like electric, nerves, anxiety. It was definitely a different feeling. Still an awful feeling, but just different." Riley felt frustrated that she couldn't pinpoint the difference.

Eve said, "All of the mill dogs were small dogs. Did these dogs sound large or small?"

Riley closed her eyes and thought about it. "Both," she said. "Most of them sounded larger, but I know I heard some smaller ones too."

"Do you think it's another puppy mill somewhere?" Finn asked.

Riley thought for a moment. "I mean, I don't know. I didn't see a ton of detail-" She cut herself off and looked at Finn. "Emily said Baby Girl was a rescue, right?" Finn nodded. "Well, if she came from a reputable rescue group, she would be spayed."

Finn knew what she meant. "You're right. They wouldn't have a need for a spayed dog at a puppy mill."

"And," Eve said, "Baby Girl isn't a pure-bred dog, and that's what a puppy miller would want."

Frustrated she couldn't figure out more, Riley fiddled with the key she and Finn found in the cellar of the Public House that she wore as a necklace. She wore it all the time now. It reminded her of Mister Oscar, the slave ghost who clearly looked out for her, so she wore it for luck. "You're right, a puppy mill wouldn't make any sense."

"What else did you feel?" Finn asked.

Riley inhaled then exhaled and absentmindedly put her hands on her own neck. "I felt a tightness on my neck and shoulders. It was aggressive." She swore she could feel her stomach flip as she thought back to the next sensation. "Then, I felt all these sharp things hitting my face. Hard."

Finn and Eve listened with their mouths agape. "What do you think that was?" Finn asked. "Do you think she was just lost and scared? Maybe she got into a scrape with a stray dog?"

Riley shook her head and frowned. "No, it wasn't that innocent. It was like I was being bombarded with bee stings, but harder, way harder." She thought for a moment and unconsciously touched her face. "I did notice marks on Baby Girl's face that weren't in the pictures of her before she got lost."

"Maybe she was in the woods and got caught in some brambles?" Finn suggested.

"No!" Riley said as she paced along the wooden porch. She stopped herself and looked at Finn earnestly, "I'm sorry." She inhaled deeply. "This was bad. This wasn't some lost-in-the-woods scenario." She recalled the sensation and put her hand over her heart. "I thought..." she paused and looked at her friends. "It felt like I was going to die."

Sadness washed across Eve's face. " Do you think someone was abusing her?"

Riley felt sick just thinking about it. "I don't know. I

didn't see a prominent presence of a person." She looked at Finn, "Like when I saw what Molly had to show me. I clearly saw a man in a hat hurt her. This time, I felt a presence of a person or people, but not as strong. I heard voices, but couldn't make out what they were saying." She started pacing again.

"That's so crazy," Finn said. "I'm sorry you had to experience that. For what it's worth, you seemed to recover pretty well in there."

Riley turned it all over in her head and thought about the one figure she did see clearly. "After the bad stuff, I had a sense of peace wash over me. I saw a little boy in a home and Baby Girl was with him. That's when I felt peaceful and comfortable."

"That must have been Baby Girl showing you when she got back to her family, finally being at home and letting you know she's safe now," Eve said.

"Yeah, I think so," Riley said and felt comfort in knowing that the sweet dog was safe again. "Thanks for taking notes, Eve. When I get home, I'm going to write this all down in as much detail as I can and think back to everything I saw."

"Good idea," Finn said. "You might remember stuff when you're alone and focused." He looked at his watch. "It's about time to pack up. Let's see if our parents are back."

With that, the kids headed back down the porch steps and over to their table where most of the volunteers gathered. Riley welcomed all the help breaking everything down. As scary as it would be to relive what Baby Girl had shown her, Riley really wanted to try and figure out what she had been through in those long months when she was gone. There had to be some sort of detail that would help her figure this out. Her nerves fluttered as she thought about the experience that poor dog went through.

"The clue!" Finn said as he picked up one of the fans from the chiropractic office and put it in a box with all their brochures.

"Oh my gosh," Riley said. "With all the Baby Girl stuff, I almost forgot."

"Me too," Eve said. "Maybe we can have a sleepover tomorrow night and work on the clue and the Baby Girl stuff?"

"Great idea!" Riley said. "I'll ask my parents if it's okay. I'm sure it will be." While the second clue they had found in *Gone with the Wind* excited Riley, she wasn't as excited to think about what Baby Girl had shown her. Just thinking about it made her stomach flutter with nerves.

CHAPTER NINE

Sleepover Prep

Riley was so glad Friday had arrived and that she and her friends had the freedom of the weekend. Riley couldn't wait for summer break when they would have more time together. She relished summer, mostly because she didn't have to get up early or do any homework. Riley's mom loved any opportunity to entertain, and since she was a stay-at-home mom, she had spent the afternoon grocery shopping and prepping for Riley's sleepover.

"Thanks for doing all of this, mom. You didn't have to go to any trouble," Riley said as she helped her mom roll little hot dogs into pastry dough.

"Oh honey, it's no problem," her mom said. "I enjoy doing stuff like this. In fact, with you girls being so independent now, I'm thinking of doing some volunteer work."

"Cool. What are you thinking about doing?" Riley asked her mom as she glanced under the kitchen table and saw their dog Buster watching the activity from one of his safe spaces. He was still learning how to be a family dog.

Her mom looked as perfect as ever. Her blond hair didn't have a strand out of place, her face perfectly made-up, and her manicure looked fresh and on-point. She smoothed a delicate hand over her eggshell blue apron and said, "Well, the Women's Club is great, but we only meet once a month, and I have more time to give. I'm thinking of possibly volunteering to be a docent at one of the historic homes in Roswell."

Riley's eye grew wide. "That would be awesome, mom! Those homes have so much history!"

Riley's mom gave her a knowing look. "I know, and you and Finn would just love to have private access to do some ghost hunting, I'm sure." She winked a pretty blue eye at her daughter and smiled.

Riley grinned. "Well, if you're offering, we'd totally take you up on that!"

"I can't believe you and Finn still do that." Riley's older sister Hailey had walked in on their conversation. "I mean, have you actually gotten any real evidence of anything?"

Riley hated how her sister always acted so condescending toward everything she did. She figured it must be an older sister thing, but hated it nonetheless. "We've captured several things, as a matter of fact," Riley said trying to remain calm. She would never consider telling her about Mister Oscar, the spirit that had saved her life, or her ability to 'see' what dogs wanted to communicate with her. Riley worked hard to not let her sister's attitude and comments bother her so much. It could be really hard sometimes.

"It just seems so boring," Hailey said as she grabbed a slice of cheese that their mom had cut and sauntered over to the sofa.

"Well," Riley said, "it's way more interesting than reading

gossip magazines or watching reality television."

"Whatever," Hailey said as she picked up an aforementioned gossip magazine and started flipping through it.

Riley knew she had won this argument for a change and felt proud of herself. She looked at her mom and said, "Which house do you think you'd like to work at most?"

Her mom put the baking sheet with the pigs-in-a-blanket in the oven. "I'll work wherever they need me, though I do think Bulloch Hall would be fun. You know, since it has presidential history and all."

"Really?" Riley asked as she took a piece of cheese her mom had sliced.

"Yep," Riley's mom said as her eyes sparkled. "Mittie Bulloch married Theodore Roosevelt, Sr. in the dining room at Bulloch Hall, and their son, was Theodore Roosevelt our twenty-sixth president."

"That's cool," Riley said, but changed to a topic that interested her a bit more. "Well, there are definitely stories of that house being haunted," she said. Just then, the doorbell rang. Buster started barking as he hopped up from his safe space and headed to the front door. "That must be them!" Riley said as she followed Buster.

Riley opened the front door to see her best friend's smiling face. As Finn stepped into the Carson's foyer, Riley and Finn heard Eve's brother's truck rumble up the street. Riley waved at Eve and Evan as the truck pulled into their driveway. After a moment, Eve hopped out with a bag in hand and headed up to the porch. "Hey guys!"

"Hey," Riley and Finn said in unison.

"Come on in," Riley said as she led her friends into the kitchen.

After the kids greeted Mrs. Carson and Hailey, they grabbed some of the food Riley's mom prepared and headed into the nicely finished basement. It served as another level of living space for the family. The basement included a small kitchen area stocked with drinks for the kids, a game area, living area, a full bathroom, and a storage area. The kids put the snacks on the coffee table, and Riley went to grab drinks from the mini-fridge. As she pulled out bottles of water, she heard Buster slowly make his way down the stairs, proud of him since they were still new to him. "Good boy!" she said in a high voice as her little Yorkie trotted over to her. She petted him, and then she headed to the couches with him following behind. Riley smiled as Buster made himself comfy underneath the coffee table.

"So," Eve asked tentatively, "have you figured out any more about what Baby Girl showed you?"

Riley inhaled a deep breath and then exhaled before she spoke. "I wrote it all down and included every detail I could think of. It was really tough. I felt so much fear and anxiety from Baby Girl, but I still can't figure out what happened to her. I've been thinking about it ever since it happened."

"So, it wasn't as clear a picture as what you've seen from other dogs?" Finn asked.

"Exactly," Riley said. "It was more emotions than images which made it tough. All I know is that she was really scared and went through a lot."

Eve could sense how tough this was for Riley, after all,

she was able to see ghosts herself and had even seen Mister Oscar and knew he was hanging around to protect them. "Since you've already spent so much time trying to figure that out, why don't we focus on the clue tonight."

Riley immediately relaxed her shoulders and said, "That sounds like a great idea. If it's okay with you guys, I'd rather put the Baby Girl thing aside, at least for tonight."

Of course, her friends agreed, and instead, they set out to decipher this most recent clue from the Powell's copy of *Gone with the Wind*.

CHAPTER TEN

Clue Solved?

Eve pulled the copy of *Gone with the Wind* out of her bag and settled back onto the sofa. She flipped the pages until they opened at a spot where Eve placed a plain white envelope. "Here's the newest clue," Eve said as she opened the envelope and took out a small piece of paper. "Maybe we should discuss what we think this could mean and go over it line by line?"

Riley and Finn agreed. "Can I see it again?" Riley asked. After Eve handed Riley the clue, she read it aloud,

"Sacred words are written within. While there are many versions, there is no twin. Our family tree runs very deep. If I lost this book, I would surely weep."

The kids took out notebooks, and each of them wrote down the clue. In between bites of a pig-in-a-blanket, Finn said, "Obviously this book is really important to this person, because it contains sacred words."

Riley agreed, "Yeah, I think that's really important. Probably the most important part of the clue."

"And, if the clue writer lost this book, they would be really sad," Eve said referring to the last line of the clue.

Finn grabbed another snack. "And we know it's not the

55

only book because there are many versions."

"But," Riley said, "it's unique in some way because there isn't a twin. That part has me confused." She leaned forward and grabbed a snack as she thought about this clue.

"Do you think it's a book about this person's family?" Finn asked. "That third line seems kind of out of place, but it wouldn't be in the clue if it weren't important."

"Unless the purpose is to throw us off a bit," Riley suggested.

Eve said, "If it's about the clue writer's family, then maybe it's a first edition with a personal and meaningful inscription inside?"

"Could be," Riley said. "If we are correct that this is Mr. Powell's book and his clues, we could ask Mrs. Powell if there were any books written about Mr. Powell's family."

"Good idea," Finn said. "In the meantime, I'll go online and see if I can find any books written about them."

As Eve leaned toward the coffee table to grab a snack, she said, "Too bad he didn't have an uncommon name."

Riley chuckled, "Yeah, seriously." She closed her notebook and grabbed more snacks as she pondered this.

Finn worked away at his computer. "I think I found something!"

Riley and Eve sat up and focused their attention on Finn. "What?" Riley asked.

"Well, I found this book online, The Story of Georgia and the Georgia People, 1732 to 1860. There's a full copy of it in the New York Public Library, and you can view the it on their website. In it is a James Powell who was in government in Georgia when the Constitution was ratified. He was from Liberty county as was James Dunwoody…that's weird." Finn cut himself off.

"What's weird?" Riley asked, curious about what Finn had found.

"Well, James Dunwoody spells his name with two o's. John Dunwody from Roswell only used one. I wonder if they are related?"

"If they are, it would make sense if they are both from the same area," Eve said. "And Liberty county is near Savannah. Didn't the Roswell founders come from that area?"

"They sure did," Riley said, excitement evident in her voice. "Did James Powell write the book you're looking at?"

Finn looked up, "I just searched 'James Powell, Roswell, book…"As Finn scrolled to the top of the page, he said, "Let me check." His expression changed as he got to the top, "Nope, this was written by George G. Smith."

"No one had unique names back then, did they?" Eve joked.

"This is kind of cool, though," Finn said. He scrolled down a bit on the page. "It was printed in Atlanta and self-published." He read aloud, "'NOTE, I am my own publisher, not of choice, but of necessity. There are no publishing houses North or South that are willing to risk the publishing of State histories by whomsoever written. I have confidence in the Georgia people and have acted in accordance with it. The book is not as fully illustrated as I would have preferred. Some handsome churches and court-houses would have appeared if the parties concerned had complied with my request for half-tones. Many have, and I am under obligations to them for the use of their plates. Vineville, Macon, Ga.'"

"People wrote really formally back then, didn't they?" Riley said. "It's kind of cool."

Eve said, "Are there any other references to Powells?"

Finn did a quick search by pressing the CTRL and F keys on his laptop. "Ugh, yep, forty-two! I'll scan through them really quickly."

While he did this, Riley said, "Let's not go too far down this rabbit hole. We need to focus on figuring out this clue." She opened her laptop to start her own search.

As Finn clicked away, he said, "Yep, this basically tells us there are a bunch of Powells in early Georgia. Why couldn't we be dealing with a name like Isaac Antrobus or T. Netherclift?"

"Are those real names?" Eve asked as she jotted in her notebook.

"Yep, real names," Finn said. "I don't think this book is going to get us anywhere. It's a lot of what it says it is; people of early Georgia." He sighed as he closed his laptop and grabbed some snacks from the table.

Riley typed something into her laptop. After a moment, she said, "I think I found something!"

"Did you find the book?" Finn asked. His blue eyes sparkled.

Riley said, "I can't believe we didn't think of this sooner. I didn't find the book, but I think I know what book we should be looking for."

"What book should we be looking for? Did someone in Mr. Powell's family write it?" Finn asked eagerly.

Riley chuckled. "I think we need to find a Bible."

"A Bible? Which one? There are so many versions!" Finn felt a little exasperated.

Eve realized something and read part of the clue to her friends, *"Our family tree runs very deep. If I lost this book, I would surely weep.* Family tree isn't about who wrote the book, it's about who wrote *in* the book!" Riley and Finn waited for Eve to explain. "I think the clue is to a family Bible."

Recognition lit Riley's face. "Yes, I think you're right! It has to be a family Bible." Finn looked a little lost so she explained. "Families used to write down important events and information in the family Bible, like births and deaths, marriages. Stuff like that."

"That's so cool!" Finn said. "So, now we need to find Mr. Powell's family Bible?"

Eve smiled. "I think so! Riley, can you see if we can go to Mrs. Powell's tomorrow?"

Riley looked at the clock on her computer. "Yeah, but I think I'll call in the morning. I don't want to disturb her this late."

Finn grabbed his laptop again and clicked away. "It says that family Bibles also sometimes contained letters and photographs. I hope that means the Powell family Bible contains another clue."

"Me too." Riley said as she closed her laptop and grabbed her drink. She appreciated this distraction, but her time with Baby Girl slipped back into her mind and made her uneasy.

She knew she would have to spend some time reflecting on this but wasn't ready to yet. She feared she might even have to try to see Baby Girl again if she wanted to figure it out at all.

CHAPTER ELEVEN

Clue Hunting with Mrs. Powell

Riley and her friends were so excited about going to see Mrs. Powell, that they stayed up late imagining what they might find in the Powell family Bible. After a delicious breakfast cooked by both her parents, Riley called Mrs. Powell. As usual, she said she would be delighted if they came over, and of course, the dogs were welcome too.

When they arrived at the pretty antebellum home on Mimosa Street, Riley, Finn, Eve, Buster, and Molly climbed the porch steps. Riley pressed the doorbell. They immediately heard Lily barking to let Mrs. Powell know that the doorbell had just rung and this made Riley smile. Buster whined a little upon hearing Lily, and Molly wagged her tail. It appeared the dogs were excited about today too.

After Mrs. Powell greeted them, she led them into the sitting room off the left of the foyer. "So," she said, "tell me what you have found in that old copy of *Gone with the Wind*?" Mrs. Powell looked as eager as Riley felt to solve the clues to this fun mystery.

Eve pulled the large tome from her backpack and opened it to where the envelope was nestled. She removed the clue and handed it to Mrs. Powell. "Here it is. Unfortunately, the class bully grabbed it from us and dropped it. The book's spine cracked, and that's when we found this."

Mrs. Powell looked at the book and said, "Oh don't you worry. That book is yours to keep, and as you can tell from its condition to begin with, it didn't hold much value." She smiled at the kids. "Besides, *Gone with the Wind* is a staple in these parts since Margaret Mitchell was from Atlanta. I could easily find another one, but I've already read it."

Mrs. Powell took the small paper from Eve and read to herself. When she finished reading, she lowered the paper and looked at the kids with a smile. "Well, I can see why you said on the phone that you wanted to look at the family Bible. The words in the Bible are sacred, and there are so many versions of the Bible but not an exact replica of the one the clue writer is referencing. A family Bible would be different from every other version and, if lost, it would be tragic due to the history recorded inside. I'm impressed!" Her blue eyes grew wide as she looked at Riley and her friends.

Riley smiled proudly. "It was definitely a team effort! Thanks for letting us look at Mr. Powell's Bible."

Mrs. Powell smiled sweetly and nodded to the settee. "Please have a seat, and I'll get the Bible." She looked at the well-behaved dogs, still on their leashes and sniffing one another. "And you can take off those leashes. They'll be fine to roam around."

Riley and Finn unclipped their dogs' leashes as Mrs. Powell headed across the foyer and into the library. After a moment, she returned with a well-worn Bible. "Do you know what you're looking for?"

Eve said, "We're hoping there's a clue tucked inside or written on one of the pages." As she said this, she glanced at the thick book and recalled how thin pages in her own Bible were. "Hopefully it's somewhat easy to find."

"If it's anything like the last clue, it might not be," Riley said. "But surely with this delicate book, it's not hidden away like the last clue."

Mrs. Powell absentmindedly rubbed her hand across the cover. She smiled and said, "Do you know why family Bibles were so important?"

Finn said, "Yeah, Riley explained them to me last night, because I didn't know much about them, and then I did some research. Didn't families record important events and even tuck deeds, letters, and photos in the pages?"

"That's right," Mrs. Powell said. "Before there were computers and record-keeping systems, this was it." She patted the Bible when she said this. "Why do you think the Bible was used for this?"

The kids thought about what she asked them. Riley said, "Well, the Bible would be very important, and if there was a fire or a storm, you would keep the Bible with you, wouldn't you?"

Mrs. Powell's eyes crinkled around the edges as she smiled. "That's right, Riley. This book had all the important stuff inside and would be the first thing that a family would take with them in an emergency."

"The sacred words and all their history," Eve said.

Mrs. Powell nodded and said, "I haven't looked through this in a while, but I know that James' family was very diligent at recording their history. In fact, this Bible dates back to before the Civil War."

"Wow," Finn said. "From what I read online, that means it must be worth a lot."

"I would say it's priceless," Mrs. Powell said with a wink. She carefully opened the pages. "What are we looking for?"

"Well," Eve offered, "since the last clue was on a piece of paper, I think we should look for something that might be tucked inside. I doubt Mr. Powell would have written a clue directly on the pages of something so important."

"That's a good thought," Mrs. Powell said as she gently leafed through the pages. "There are a few old photographs of family members who I probably won't remember..." She continued to gently flip the pages and stopped about halfway through the book. "Here's something." She gently removed a yellowed piece of paper and unfolded it twice. A sweet smile appeared as she read aloud, "My true love, I will cherish you 'till the end of our days. All my love, Lucy Mae."

"Is that a love note from you?" Riley said sweetly.

Mrs. Powell's eyes were misty as she admired the note and nodded her head. "I wrote this for James on our wedding day, and had his best man tuck it into his pocket."

"And he saved it all those years!" Eve said.

"That's so special," Riley said.

"He was a wonderful man," Mrs. Powell said, but then grew more serious. "But, you aren't here to find my old love notes! Let me keep looking."

Riley could tell their friend was having fun with this, and she enjoyed a stroll down memory lane with Mrs. Powell. She looked at the floor and saw Buster under Mrs. Powell's coffee table while Lily and Molly stretched out on either side of Mrs. Powell. They clearly knew whose house this was.

As she neared the end of the book, Mrs. Powell said, "I don't see any other notes or pages tucked in here. Just some old photos. We may have to look for something hand-written. I'll start at the front where all the births, deaths, and such are listed."

Riley thought about where the clue could be within the book as Mrs. Powell looked at the notes in the front, then the back. "Everything I'm seeing here is historical about the Powell family. I'm afraid I don't see anything that looks like a clue," Mrs. Powell said. She got out of her chair and walked over to the settee where Riley and Finn sat. "Let's look together," she said as she sat down between them. She looked at Eve who occupied the other chair across from them. "Eve come over here and see if you can help us."

Since the settee was set away from the windows that looked out onto the front porch, it allowed room for Eve to stand behind them, which she happily did. Mrs. Powell showed the kids the records of births and deaths in the front of the Bible, and then showed them the notes in the back. After carefully going over everything, they couldn't find any sort of clue.

"What about the pictures?" Eve asked. "Maybe there's a clue in them?"

Mrs. Powell flipped to the pages with photos and showed them to the kids. "I'm afraid they're mostly just old photographs of old relatives," Mrs. Powell said as they looked at a picture of a very serious-looking and unsmiling bearded man.

"Isn't it funny how people didn't smile at cameras way back then?" Finn said. "Yeah," Eve said as she inspected the stern faces looking at them. "They always look so serious."

"When photography was new, it was formal and it wasn't in fashion to smile," Mrs. Powell explained as they looked at a photograph with jagged, pinked edges. "This one is much more recent. This was Mr. Powell and his family." She pointed to a handsome young man with a crew cut wearing a white t-shirt and dark blue jeans. "That's James."

"He was so cute!" Riley said.

Mrs. Powell's tone became reminiscent. "Oh, he was. All the girls wanted to date James, but he was never really interested in all of that. He was more interested in exploring and history. I don't think he was aware of the girls, and I ended up being the lucky one."

Riley tried to imagine Mrs. Powell as a young girl. She wondered what life must have been like, and how much she had seen in her years. "Is it crazy to you that you saw the invention of the television, the internet and everything in between?"

Mrs. Powell looked at Riley and smiled. "It's quite amazing what I've seen and how fast technology has advanced. I just hope I'm not around when robots take over!" Mrs. Powell made them all laugh at this.

As Mrs. Powell showed the kids a few more photographs, none of which appeared to contain a clue, Riley had a thought. "Mrs. Powell? Isn't there a section in the Bible attributed to James?"

"Great idea!" Eve said. "The letter of James!"

Mrs. Powell smiled and said, "Good thinking. Let's check there." She carefully turned the delicate pages to the very back of the book. "It's rather short, so we won't have to look too terribly long." As she turned to the section with James' epistle, there was a photograph marking it. "Here's a picture right where James starts." The photo was in black and white and captured Roswell's town square. "Oh, I remember when we took this one."

"Gosh, it looked so different back then," Eve said as she looked at the picture showing classic cars with rounded sides and lots of chrome parked in front of the buildings on Atlanta Street. "I guess they had less traffic then, because now it's four lanes and no parking in front of those buildings."

"That's so cool," Finn said as he moved in to take a closer look. "The picture doesn't look like a clue, though, does it?"

Riley leaned in now too. "Nope, just a cool old picture."

Mrs. Powell set the picture aside and said, "Let's see if there's anything on these pages." Riley could tell she was getting excited about finding another clue too. Mrs. Powell scanned the first well-worn page, running her wrinkled index finger down the page as she searched. "Nothing out of the ordinary here," she said as she turned to the next page. They slowly looked at each page for any tiny clue or markings anywhere, but there wasn't a thing.

"Can I see that picture again?" Riley asked. Mrs. Powell handed her the picture. Riley inspected it closely and didn't see any sort of clue in the photograph, so she turned it over. Mrs. Powell had turned over a few of the older pictures to determine who was in them. While they didn't need to know the information about the picture, Riley thought it was worth looking...and her instinct paid off. "Look! There's a series of numbers here! It's tiny, but it's something," she said hopefully.

Riley pointed to a faint series of numbers written in the bottom corner and handed the picture to Mrs. Powell. "With these old eyes, I would never have seen that," Mrs. Powell said with a smile and moved the photo further away from her aging eyes and squinted.

Finn moved to the edge of his seat and tapped his phone a couple of times. "Read me the numbers."

Mrs. Powell handed the photograph back to Riley who read the small series of numbers, " 220-17-14."

"Definitely not a date," Eve said.

"Nope," Finn said as he chewed on his thumbnail. He sat up straight and said to Mrs. Powell, "Can we check the rest of the pictures to see if there is anything like this on them?"

"Of course," the older lady said as she put the photograph right back where she found it. She gently turned the pages to another photo they already looked at. This one showed a handsome, young Mr. Powell and his family. Mrs. Powell turned the picture over and squinted hard. "Well I'll be. Would you look at that!" In tiny, faint handwriting appeared another series of numbers which she read to Finn. "26-15-5-6." She showed the picture to Riley and said, "Make sure I got it right."

Riley read the numbers again, "Yep, you got it!" She jokingly poked Mrs. Powell in the arm, "See, your eyes aren't that bad." The old lady chuckled, and her eyes wrinkled around the edges as her mouth curved up in a smile. Riley could tell she enjoyed this too!

They found seven pictures in all, and each one had tiny, faint numbers. Eve said, "It's weird. There's only one that has a series of four numbers. The rest are a series of three."

"Oh yeah," Finn said as he looked at his notes. "Nice catch, but what do you guys think these mean?"

"I don't know. Maybe they refer to scripture?" Riley offered.

Mrs. Powell reviewed the numbers Finn recorded. "I don't know. These numbers don't seem to fit how scriptures are numbered."

Eve jotted the numbers down in her notebook. She chewed on her pen cap as she thought it over. "We know they aren't dates because none of these have years, and some of them start with a two-digit number, and the rest start with three-digit numbers."

Riley looked at Eve's notebook with her. "And the second and third numbers, plus the one fourth, are much smaller. The highest one is fifty."

Finn looked at his notes. "And the last numbers are small with the largest one being fourteen."

Riley inhaled, and then exhaled. "Just when you think you're onto something, there's another mystery to solve!"

Mrs. Powell smiled sweetly and patted Riley's knee. "Isn't that the fun of life, though?"

Riley returned the smile. "It sure is. We love this stuff! Thank you so much for helping us find these clues."

"Of course, dear. This was fun!" Mrs. Powell said. "I just hope you can figure out what all those crazy numbers actually mean."

CHAPTER TWELVE

Codes, Clues, and Ciphers, Oh My!

Riley, Finn, and Eve had spent the afternoon researching codes, clues, and ciphers, but by dinner time, they still hadn't figured out what the numbers they found could mean. After a delicious meal with her family, Riley and her friends headed back to the basement with renewed energy to solve this newest clue.

As they walked down the staircase, Finn said, "I can't believe you forgot to tell us that your mom is going to be a docent at one of the historic homes."

"I know! I was so excited about the clues, I totally forgot." Riley said enthusiastically. "Once she finds out where she'll be and has settled in, I'll ask her if we can come hang out. She's already said she expects us to want to ghost hunt."

"That's cool," Eve said softly, but Riley could tell she wasn't as excited about it as she and Finn were.

Riley smiled kindly at Eve. "I can imagine you wouldn't want to go ghost hunting with us, but you're always invited."

Eve smiled at Riley. "Thanks. And, thanks for understanding."

"Okay," Finn said as he sat on the sofa and opened his laptop. "Let's crack this code!"

Riley felt excited to figure out this clue and even more excited that her parents and her friends' parents all agreed to another slumber party. Riley figured since it was almost the end of the school year, their parents decided to go easy on them.

"Am I just a huge nerd, or are ciphers kinda cool?" Eve asked.

Finn laughed. "Regardless of what Corey says, you're not a nerd." The mention of Corey's name made Riley groan as Eve giggled. "They are pretty cool, but man, some of the stuff I'm finding is so complicated!"

"There's so much on this topic," Riley said as she scanned an article on her laptop. "There's even an American Cryptogram Association, and they list all kinds of ciphers on their website."

"It would be cool to really learn about this, but I just want to figure out what these numbers mean right now," Finn said.

"I know," Eve said. "Why couldn't we have found something easy like a Pigpen cipher?"

"What's that?" Riley asked as she looked at Eve.

Eve turned her computer so Riley could see. "It's pretty easy and cool because it uses symbols for letters. So, you have a key like this." Eve pointed to a grid with the alphabet written inside it, in alphabetical order. Next to it was the same grid, but each of the squares had a letter and a dot inside. That got you from 'A' through 'R'. Below that were two 'X's with letters inside the first one, 'S' through 'V', then one with dots and letters finishing out the alphabet with 'W' through 'Z'. "And for each letter you want to use, you draw the shape around the letter.

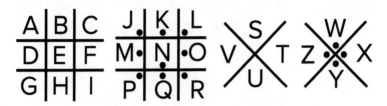

Eve continued, "So, 'A' would be like this." She grabbed her pad and pen and drew a straight line down, then a line off to the left of the bottom of the first line, like a backwards 'L.'

"And 'C' would be like this." Finn took the pad and pen, then drew the same shape, but this time it looked like a regular 'L'.

"Cool," Riley said. "So, 'E' would be a square?"

"Yep," Eve said. "Since the 'E' is in the middle of the grid, you would indicate it as a square.

"And," Finn added, "so you don't get confused with the letter 'N,' it's in the center of the grid, but its grid has dots, so 'N' would be a square with a dot above the bottom line, in the direct center."

"That's so cool!" Riley said. "If we had found a clue like that, we may not have understood it at first, but I bet we would have found this pretty quickly. Let me test it out." She grabbed Eve's pad and pen, then drew the following:

Riley showed the page to her friends. "Can you decipher this?"

Eve looked at the page, then smiled. "That's my name!"

"Yep." Riley said, smiling. "This is pretty cool!"

"It says here that it's a pretty simple cipher and is primarily used in children's books and secret writing," Eve said.

"Look!" Finn spotted something exciting on Eve's screen. "It says that General Washington used a version that had a more random layout of the letters. And that Confederate and Union soldiers used it in prisons."

Riley grew excited now too. "That's so cool! I really want to find out what our numbers mean." She turned back to her own computer and kept researching as her friends did the same.

After a while, she said, "You guys! I think I've found something." Riley sat up straight and her friends listened intently. "I did a search for 'Civil War Ciphers' after you said that Union and Confederate soldiers used the Pigpen cipher to send messages and I found some stuff about dictionary code. They would use a dictionary to create the code, and it contained numbers for the page, line, and word in the sentence."

"No way!" Finn said as he sat up straight now too.

Riley continued, "If you and I had the same, exact book, I could give you a series of numbers, and you could use your copy of the book to decipher my code. If the code was intercepted, no one would know what it meant unless they knew which book we had previously agreed to use as the key. All they would have is a set of numbers, just like what we have now." Riley saw recognition in her friends' eyes.

"Oh my gosh," Eve said. "That's genius!"

"I know," Riley said quickly as she glanced back at her screen. "It says here that a common book was used. One that wouldn't seem out of place in a person's possession." She looked up at her friends and smiled. "In fact, the Bible was often used for this."

Finn's eyes grew wide. "Mr. Powell's Bible!" Finn typed furiously on his computer. "Okay, so I searched 'Bible cipher,' and the first result is 'Book cipher.'" He scanned the website. "Yep, it shows dictionary code and Bible cipher. The dictionary code assures all words would be in the book and would be pretty easy because all you would need is a page number and line number."

Eve said, "But our code has three numbers per line, and one has four."

"That's why I'm thinking it's the Bible!" Finn said. "The first number would be the page number, the second number would be the line number, and the third number would be the word on that line!"

"But what about the one that has four numbers?" Eve asked.

Finn thought about it. "Maybe that one has two words on the same line?"

Eve raised her eyebrows. "Good thought. We need to take a look at that Bible again!"

Riley wasn't so sure. "Hang on guys. All of this stuff was used by spies. It was used to hide messages. Why would you put the code in the book that held the answers?"

Finn's shoulders sagged. "She's right. No good spy would leave the clues in the code book. Even though he wasn't a spy, I doubt Mr. Powell would have put the clues in the code book."

"Yeah, you're probably right," Eve said disappointedly.

Riley hated bursting their bubbles. "We can always ask Mrs. Powell to look at the Bible again, but I don't think it's it. It will be a large book with lots of words in it, because that's what spies use. A book that's likely to have the words you need and lots of them."

"Like the dictionary," Finn said. "I can really see why that gets used."

Eve pondered aloud, "A large book with lots of words..."

Riley added, "That the clue writer and the receiver would have access to..."

It was as if they all realized it at the same time. "*Gone with the Wind*!" they said in unison.

CHAPTER THIRTEEN

Clue Solved!

Riley and her friends were on pins and needles as Eve pulled the worn copy of *Gone with the Wind* out of her backpack. Finn said, "I'll read off the numbers so you can find the words." Riley looked at her notebook where she had written down the numbers for reference.

220-17-14

679-32-6

501-46-3

26-15-5-6

304-28-9

441-50-3

2-20-1

"Sounds like a plan," Eve said.

"I'll write everything down," Riley said.

"Okay," Finn said. "The first one is 220-17-14." Riley was hunched over her notebook, had her pen ready, and watched in anticipation as Eve flipped the pages of the old book.

Eve arrived at page 220, then counted down to line seventeen, then across to the fourteenth word. "Tunnels! The first word is tunnels!" She looked up at her friends, her amber eyes aglow.

Riley felt so excited, and Finn jumped up, his eyes like saucers. "Oh my gosh, this has to be the right book!" She wrote down the word 'tunnels'.

Finn hurried to get the next word, "Next is 679-32-6."

Eve quickly turned to page 679, counted down to line 32, then across to the sixth word. "Used."

"Okay," Finn said as he sat back down on the sofa. "The next one is 501-46-3."

Eve turned to page 501 then asked, "Forty-six?"

"Yeah," Finn said as he double checked. "Then three."

Eve counted down then across, "Treasure!"

"No way," Riley said as she leaned in to look.

Eve sat in between Riley and Finn who both squeezed in to see for themselves. Sure enough, Eve's pencil tip was on the word 'treasure.'

"Oh my gosh!" Finn said. His eyes danced with excitement. "The next one is the four-digit code, 26-15-5-6."

Eve turned from the back of the book to the front and found page twenty-six. "To help," she said.

Riley wrote down the words as Finn said, "Next is 304-28-9."

Eve quickly turned to page 304 and counted. "Hide! The next word is hide."

"This is so exciting." Riley felt like she could climb out of her skin.

"Next is 441-50-3," Finn said moving along quickly.

Eve did her thing and turned to the back of the book again. "Confederate! The next word is Confederate."

"One more word," Finn said. "2-20-1."

Eve turned to the very front of the book, counted down twenty lines and looked at the first word. Seeing it always kind of stung. "Slaves. The last word is slaves."

Riley focused on the chain of words she wrote, and they weren't what she expected. She read aloud to her friends. "Tunnels used treasure to help hide Confederate slaves." She looked at her friends with confusion. "How could tunnels use treasure?"

Finn thought for a moment. "Maybe they used treasure to build the tunnels?"

"Just so they could hide slaves?" Eve asked. "I doubt it. Why would they use their treasure to build something just to hide slaves?"

Riley shifted uncomfortably in her seat. She considered how to respectfully say what she was thinking to her friend who likely had ancestors who were slaves in the South. "Um, well, wouldn't they want to protect their slaves because if it weren't for the slaves, they wouldn't have people to do the work? I mean, they were like a commodity to them." Riley sighed in frustration and tucked her hair behind her ear. "Gosh, I hate even saying that."

Eve thought about it. "I totally get what you're saying, but wouldn't there have been other places to hide slaves? Heck, even a root cellar or something. And, besides, I don't really think anyone was hiding slaves back then."

Riley nodded. "Yeah, good point."

"I think you're right," Finn said. "Think about it, tunnels are used to go places or move things." He looked at Riley. "I think Eve's right. I don't think they would have built tunnels to hide slaves."

Riley bit on her thumbnail as she thought. "It's weird. The language used here; it just doesn't sound right."

"How do you mean?" Finn asked.

Riley sat up. "Well, everything we've read from Mr. Powell has been pretty eloquent. He used good grammar. Why all of a sudden would he use words like this?" Finn tilted his head up and looked at the ceiling, turning this thought over.

"So, what if these words are in the wrong order?" Finn suggested as recognition spread across his face.

Riley bounced up in her seat. "Like a word jumble!"

"Yes!" Finn said. "When we looked at the photos in the Powell family Bible, did we write down the code numbers in order of how they were laid out in the book?"

"No!" Eve said. "Remember, we noticed the first code on the picture of The Square in the section from James. That was toward the end."

"She's right." Riley said, excited again. She looked at the time. "I'll call Mrs. Powell. It's still early enough." As she dialed Mrs. Powell, Riley's friends sat by with eager expressions focused on her, they were all buzzing with anticipation.

After Riley explained how they deciphered the meaning of the numbered code, Mrs. Powell's lively voice came through the speaker. "Oh, that sounds like my James!" Riley smiled at her friends as they listened. It was as if they could hear Mrs. Powell smiling as she spoke.

Riley explained that she needed the numbers in the same order as the photographs appeared in the Bible. As she listened to Mrs. Powell, she wrote a number next to each of the lines of code in her notebook. Once she and Mrs. Powell went through each one, Riley read the words in their new order, "It says, 'Slaves used tunnels to help hide Confederate treasure!'"

"That's so awesome," Finn said. A smile spread broadly across his face.

"That sounds more like it," Eve said with a smile of satisfaction.

Riley said into her phone, "Thanks so much, Mrs. Powell. Now we just need to find out more about these tunnels."

Their old friend replied, "I'll do some asking around to see what I can find. Oh, what fun this has been!"

After they said goodbye to Mrs. Powell, the kids planned what to do next.

"What if there's still treasure in the tunnels?" Finn asked.

"That would be so cool," Eve said.

Finn said, "I think the first thing we need to do is go to the Public House in the morning and see if Mr. Wood will let us explore what looks to be a tunnel off his cellar."

Riley agreed. "Yeah, since the one we had access to from the cook house at Smith Plantation has been locked up, that's really our only way in - if it's connected." Riley thought back to the feelings she had in the tunnels and fidgeted with the key necklace she always wore.

Finn gave Riley a knowing look. "Are you okay to go back in?"

Riley nodded. "Of course. Now that we know there's treasure down there, we have to take a look." She turned toward Eve. "How about you?"

Eve shifted in her seat. "I don't know. Maybe you guys explore first and let me know if you feel anything weird."

Riley nodded solemnly. "I totally understand. I just hate to go treasure hunting without you. After all, you helped us with all these clues."

Eve smiled. "I'll think about it. You two do some recon and let me know!"

"Wow, you make it sound like a legit mission!" Finn said.

Eve smiled, "Well, my dad is a cop."

The three friends laughed together. Riley felt so excited about the prospect of finding treasure, that her uneasiness with the tunnels faded quickly. She imagined just what they might find in the dusty tunnels below their city and how cool it would be to find hidden Confederate treasure.

CHAPTER FOURTEEN

Signs

Surprisingly, the kids got to sleep fairly early so they could get a jump on the day. Sunday mornings were quiet and since the Public House was on the way to Eve's house, the three walked over together. As they headed out of Riley and Finn's neighborhood and onto Mimosa Street, Riley pointed to a sign on a post. "On no, another lost dog." She took a picture of the sign with her phone.

"It looks like a new sign," Finn said as he looked at the small fluffy dog in the picture. "I haven't seen it before, and it's not faded."

"I always hate seeing Lost Dog signs," Riley said. "I always think of how worried the family must be."

"I know," Eve said. "It must be awful."

A slight coolness still hung in the air which would be gone come July. "I can't believe we figured out the clues," Riley said as they walked down the sidewalk. "What an awesome adventure this is."

Finn agreed. "To think that Eve got that book from Mrs. Willnow back when you two got detention, and it's led us on this hunt is pretty cool."

"Mr. Powell seems like he was a fun guy," Eve said.

"I know. I wish we could have met him," Riley said.

"I keep thinking about how extensive those tunnels might be," Finn said.

"Wouldn't it be so cool if we found actual treasure?" Riley said as she thought about what might be hidden away. "If the people here were worried about the Union soldiers stealing their valuables, we might even find jewelry."

Eve said, "That would be so neat."

"I would just like to find something valuable," Finn said. "Like old coins or something. It doesn't have to be gold bars."

As they turned left onto Park Square Court, Finn said, "Dang, another one." He pointed to another 'Lost Dog' sign on a sign post.

"Oh no!" Riley said as she pulled out her phone and snapped a picture. "This one is bigger. Looks kind of like a lab mix."

"We'll have to keep an eye out," Finn said. " They seem to be lost around here so maybe we'll find them since we come this way a lot."

"I hope so," Riley said. She pushed the button at the crosswalk to get across busy Atlanta Street to where the Public House was located on the other side of the square.

When they safely crossed the street, they approached the red door to the Public House, and Riley's heart sank. She saw another sign posted, but not for a lost dog. She read the sign aloud. "Regrettably, we've had to close The Public House permanently. We appreciate the support of our patrons and the historic Roswell community."

"Oh no!" Eve said. "That's so sad."

"I know," Finn said. "Not just because we can't access the cellar, but I loved this place and Mr. Wood."

"I wonder what happened," Riley wondered aloud. "It seems so sudden."

The kids walked over to the large plate glass windows that overlooked Atlanta Street and the square. "Wow, they cleared it out fast," Riley said with her hands cupped around her eyes as she pressed up to the glass to see inside. "It looks like everything is out of there."

"This stinks," Finn said as he stood next to Riley, peering inside along with her. "I'll have my mom see if she can get in touch with Mr. Wood and find out what happened." He pulled out his phone and sent a quick text to his mom.

"Well," Riley said, "I guess we'll have to find another way into the tunnels now."

Finn groaned. "Just when I thought we were getting somewhere..."

CHAPTER FIFTEEN

Spontaneous Surveillance

Since it was early in the day, the kids decided to head to Sloan Street Park to think things through before Eve had to get home. Riley and Eve sat on the swings, just barely swinging, and Finn sat on the grass in front of them. "I can't believe the Public House is closed," Finn said as he fidgeted with a piece of grass he pulled from the ground.

"I know," Riley said, "and it must have been quick because they were just open the other day."

"What could have caused them to close so quickly?" Eve asked.

"It could be anything," Finn said as he pulled his phone out of his pocket. "My mom just texted back. She said it's news to her and that she'll try to get in touch with Mr. Wood."

"Do you think it was the ghosts?" Eve asked tentatively.

"Nah," Finn said. "Those ghosts seemed to like Mr. Wood. He went out of his way to treat them special. He wasn't scared of them."

"And," Riley added as she kicked at the mulch under her sneaker, "they never did anything bad, mean, or destructive." She noticed Finn see something behind her and looked in the same direction. Riley groaned. "I wonder what he's up to."

Eve looked behind her. "Knowing him, no good."

Relief washed over Riley. Corey hadn't seen them and had already passed the park. "It's weird that he's alone. Normally he has his crew with him."

Her friends chuckled. Finn said, "Yeah, he isn't one to go off without his biggest supporters. He must be up to something."

"You think so?" Eve asked. They watched Corey pull his phone out of his backpack and head up the street toward the cemetery while glancing suspiciously around him.

"Finn's right," Riley said. "Corey doesn't spend much time by himself. We should follow him. He looks suspicious." She hopped off her swing which caused Eve to do the same as Finn sprang to his feet.

"Doesn't he always look suspicious?" Finn asked as the trio started walking along the grass toward the monument to the mill workers.

The three friends stayed a good distance behind Corey so he wouldn't notice them. "Watch," Eve said. "He's probably going to someone's house to study, and we're over here thinking he's up to no good."

The three giggled again and watched as Corey disappeared behind a sharp curve in the road. "Let's wait back here for a minute," Riley said. "I don't want him to see us."

After a minute, they slowly rounded the curve and Riley saw Corey at the front edge of a yard surrounded by chain link fencing. "That's that crazy house with all the glass bottles hanging from the trees and the overgrown yard," she whispered to her friends.

"Isn't that the house that has the dog that ran up to the fence barking that day?" Finn asked.

"Oh yeah," Riley said quietly, remembering the encounter. "We had been at the cemetery and rode our bikes by pretty fast, and the dog charged the fence. It was a pretty dog. It just scared the heck outta me!" Riley thought about that experience and remembered something else. "And, remember I told you I saw an old lady on the porch and smiled at her, but she didn't smile back?" Finn nodded. "It kinda freaked me out."

"That's Scary Mary's house," Eve said.

Finn and Riley looked at Eve, "Who?" Finn asked.

"People call her Scary Mary. I don't know much about her, but people say she's a witch," Eve explained.

Riley's eyes grew wide. "Well, she did freak me out, and she does live really close to a cemetery." Just then, she heard barking and saw Corey lean down and pick something off the sidewalk. He had almost made it to the middle of Scary Mary's fence. They watched as Corey threw something at the dog. Riley pulled out her phone. "This time, I'm catching him in the act."

"Luckily his aim is bad," Finn said, "Otherwise, I'd be stopping him. Why's he throwing pine cones at the dog?"

"'Cause he's *so* mean. If you had seen what he did to that poor cat," Eve said, referring to the first day of middle school when she tried to stop Corey from tormenting a stray cat on the school grounds. Riley had rushed over to help and that's how they became friends.

Riley had seen enough, and just as she was about to yell at Corey, she heard a voice. "You leave my dog alone!" It was an old crackly voice and while Riley knew it belonged to a woman, she couldn't see her. The thick, overgrown yard made it hard to see much from where they stood.

Corey turned to run, but he didn't get far. He almost reached the end of the fence when the large pit-mix scaled the fence and grabbed Corey from behind. Corey cried out. The dog had Corey by the waistband of his jeans and pulled him backward. Riley kept still and recorded the scene. The old lady appeared from the side of her yard. She blocked the sidewalk ahead of Corey. The woman had a garden hoe in her hands and raised it high over her head. The gnarled, old lady with crazy white hair slammed the hoe down onto the sidewalk in front of Corey. It made Riley jump, then she could see why the dog had grabbed Corey. It had just saved Corey from being bitten by a very large snake. Riley flinched and turned away when she saw the snake squirm as it was decapitated by the old lady.

They could hear Scary Mary say, "My dog was trying to alert you. She might have just saved your life." Scary Mary patted her hip. "Good girl, Scarlett. Come on." The dog walked around the dead snake and to the old lady's side. The woman petted her dog's big, blocky head, then stooped to give it a kiss right on its forehead. She looked up at Corey who seemed to be frozen in place. Scary Mary pointed a crooked finger at him and said, "I better not see you mess with my dog ever again." With that, the lady and her dog disappeared into the thick vegetation.

"Oh my gosh!" Riley said so only her friends could hear. "That was insane."

They watched as Corey took a deep breath then ran around the snake and down the street. "I've never seen Corey run so fast. That was intense," Finn said just as quietly. "Let's go see what kind of snake it was."

Honestly, Riley just wanted to get out of there, but she stopped her video camera, pocketed her phone, and followed Finn and Eve at a safe distance. "Dang, that's a big copperhead!" Finn said. He pulled out his phone and took a couple of pictures. "That old lady is tough."

Riley shivered and said, "Eew, why do you want a picture of that?"

Eve said, "Scary Mary was right. That dog saved Corey's life. That thing could have killed him."

Riley's eyes grew wide, "Really?"

Finn nodded, "She's right. That snake really could have killed Corey. At the least, it would have made him really sick."

"Wow." Riley said the only word she could muster. As the kids turned to head back the way they came, Riley looked through an opening in the vegetation and saw the old lady on her porch, just like the first time she had seen her. Again, Riley smiled at the old lady and this time, she smiled back.

CHAPTER SIXTEEN

Exciting Confirmation

Riley looked forward to Friday because it meant more time with Buster and her friends. With each day, Buster grew more and more comfortable in their home and this made Riley's heart swell. Having spent his first four years in a dirty cage, never seeing the light of day still made Riley so sad. Every day when she left for school, she would spend extra time with him and couldn't wait to see him when she got home. After Sammy died, she really didn't think she could love another dog, but she liked to think Sammy had sent Buster to her so she could help him heal and live a happy, full life.

Riley and Finn walked home from school with a hop to their step since it was the start of the weekend.

"Have you heard anything from Mrs. Powell about the tunnels?" Finn asked.

Riley had her thumbs looped in her backpack straps as they walked down the sidewalk. "Not yet. You know, I'm actually pretty excited about the tunnels now."

"Now that we know they were used to hide treasure, how could you not be?" Finn could hardly contain his excitement about the tunnels and had been talking about them all week.

Riley laughed. "It's just so cool to think about what they were used for, and if we could find treasure, that would be awesome!"

"It would be." Finn agreed.

Riley heard her phone chiming in her bag. She got excited when she saw who it was and showed Finn the screen before answering. "Hi, Mrs. Powell!" Riley hoped she found information about the tunnels from people who had grown up in Roswell a long time ago. "I'm here with Finn. I'm going to put you on speaker."

"Hello, Finn," the sweet, old lady said through the phone. "I just know you two will want to hear what I've found out. I actually found some information about tunnels underneath Roswell."

Riley and Finn stopped walking and looked at each other. Huge smiles spread across their faces. Riley said, "We're actually just on Mimosa now, heading home from school. Would now be an okay time to stop by?"

The kids heard Lily bark once in the background, and Mrs. Powell laughed. "Oh yes, now would be a great time. Lily and I look so forward to seeing you!"

With that, the kids picked up their pace and headed to Mrs. Powell's house.

###

When Riley and Finn got to Mrs. Powell's house, she welcomed them into the sitting room where she had laid out cookies for them to enjoy. Riley and Finn sat on the old settee and Lily snuggled in between them. Mrs. Powell took a seat across from them and smiled. "I think she knows you two helped her find a new home. She just loves you so much."

Riley stroked Lily's fine, white fur. "I think she loves everyone. She's such a sweetheart."

Mrs. Powell smiled. "Almost everyone. She's still not great with men, especially men in hats."

Finn petted the dog on her small head which rested on his thigh. "That's understandable."

Riley could tell that Mrs. Powell was excited about what she had found. Her eyes alight with anticipation. "So," Riley said, "what have you found out about the tunnels?"

Mrs. Powell sat forward in her chair, a bright smile on her face. "Well, I talked to a few people who I know have been here for forever. I didn't want to go broadcasting this around, you see, but I know of a few folks who would be the most likely to have some information about where these tunnels would be. Otherwise, it would be like finding a needle in a haystack."

Riley thought back to when she and Finn tried to find another way into the tunnels, and those were her exact words to Finn.

"Did you find out anything?" Finn asked, an eager excitement danced in his eyes now.

Mrs. Powell leaned forward. "I sure did. And I think this information is good and makes sense based on the clue you deciphered."

For a moment, Riley could see Mrs. Powell as a young girl. The flash of youthfulness in her excitement about this topic was so endearing to her. "What did you find out?" Riley couldn't wait to hear.

"There's an old gentleman who still lives on Canton Street. One of the few homes that hasn't been turned into a restaurant or shop. He's spent his whole life here, longer than me, and he told me he and his friends used to play in tunnels under the city...and they are very extensive!"

"That's awesome," Finn said.

Riley's mouth fell open, and her eyes widened. "Did he say how extensive?"

Mrs. Powell nodded. "He said that the tunnels ran in between the historic homes."

Riley and Finn looked at each other in amazement. "All three homes?" Riley asked.

Mrs. Powell smiled. "At least."

"What do you mean?" Finn asked.

"Well, this man is old, and his memory may not be that sharp, but he said something about all the founders' homes and the mill."

Riley and Finn looked at each other again. "Wait, so there are tunnels that connect the founders' homes and the mill?" Finn asked.

"I can't be sure, but that's how it sounded. He was very clear that there were tunnels between the founders' homes. He recalled how he had a friend who lived in one of the homes, and that's how he knew about the tunnels."

"Wow, that's so cool!" Riley said.

"Could you imagine living in one of those homes and playing in the tunnels? How awesome!" Finn said.

Riley had a thought. "Did he say which home his friend lived in?"

Mrs. Powell's smile faded. "I asked him which home, and he said, 'Off the square.' So, I asked, 'Barrington or Bulloch.'"

Finn literally sat on the edge of his seat. "What did he say?"

"Yeah," Mrs. Powell said regretfully. "He didn't say which one. He just said, 'Yeah.' Poor man. I didn't want to make him feel bad by pressing him on it. Like I said, he's really old, older than me if you can believe that."

The kids chuckled at this, even though Riley felt disappointed that they didn't get a straight answer. "Well, he said that the founders' homes are all connected, so I guess it doesn't really matter which one it was, right?"

"I guess not," Finn said. He looked at Mrs. Powell. "Do you think his mind is clear enough that he's right about the tunnels connecting the homes?"

Mrs. Powell nodded, and a soft smile reappeared. "Oh, yes. He was very sure about that and even told me that it made sense that the homes would be connected so the families could help each other during the war." Her train of thought changed. "The memory is a funny thing. You can forget what you had for breakfast but remember a very specific, sometimes random, event from your childhood. He was very sure about playing in those tunnels, and he was certain that they went in between the founders' homes."

"That's so cool, Mrs. Powell," Riley said. "Thank you so much for finding this out for us."

"Yeah," Finn said, "we really appreciate it."

Mrs. Powell smiled. "Well, if you find the tunnels, let me know - especially if you find treasure!"

"We most definitely will," Riley said. After they shared more time with Mrs. Powell and ate several tasty cookies, Riley and Finn headed home. Riley knew what their next step would be, and she knew Finn did too.

CHAPTER SEVENTEEN

Eavesdropping

Anxious to talk to Riley's mom, Riley and Finn hurried to Riley's house. They ran up the porch steps and through the front door. Upon their arrival, Buster came out from under the coffee table. Riley scooped him up, nuzzling him and kissing the side of his face. He returned her affection with a lick on her neck. "You're such a good boy," she said as she set him down and grabbed one of his treats out of a glass jar on the kitchen island. "Sit," she told him. Buster sat and looked up at her, "Good boy!" Riley gave him the treat which he gently took from her fingers.

"Mom," Riley called out. "Are you home?" As she waited for a response, Buster sat by the back door. "Do you have to go outside?" She opened the back door which was unlocked. "That's weird," she thought.

"Hey honey." It was her mom's voice coming from the backyard.

"Oh, mom, hey! I was looking for you." Riley and Finn followed Buster out the back door and into the backyard where her mom was inspecting her plants. "What are you doing out here?"

Her mom looked frustrated. "Well, I was looking at my

hydrangeas because they aren't blooming. When I went to the nursery, they asked me when they were last pruned. I think our landscapers pruned them too late last year, and I'm not going to get any flowers."

"That stinks," Riley said as she looked around at the lush garden beds surrounding the yard which Buster investigated with his nose. "I know how you like to cut them and use those in the house."

"I do," her mom pouted. "Well, we'll see. Maybe I'll get some late blooms." She looked at Riley and Finn, "What are you two up to?"

"Well," Riley said, "we wondered when you would be starting as a docent at Bulloch Hall because we thought we could swing by and see you."

Riley's mom cocked her head and smiled. "And do a little ghost hunting?"

Finn grinned. "Well, if you insist..."

This made Riley's mom laugh. "Of course, you two can come by. I'm training this week and should be good to go by next weekend. I've been reading up on all the history, and I'll be shadowing this week. Maybe you two can be on my first tour so I have some familiar faces in the crowd."

Riley liked that idea. "That would be great!"

"Yeah, thanks Mrs. Carson," Finn said.

"Good boy," Riley's mom said to Buster who had just relieved himself outside. She looked at Riley. "I'm so glad he was easy to potty-train. He's doing great, isn't he?"

Riley smiled as the little dog trotted over to them. Riley scooped him up, and they headed to the house. "He is. I'm so glad we rescued him. It's so cool to see him gain his confidence, isn't it?"

Riley's mom smiled at Buster and scratched him on the side of his face as they walked inside. "It sure is," she cooed. "In fact, lately when it's just the two of us at home, he'll come out from underneath the coffee table."

"Really?" Riley was surprised and happy to hear this.

"Just a few times," her mom said. "I even caught him in his dog bed for a minute."

"Oh my gosh, that's awesome," Riley said. "I can't wait until he feels totally comfortable. I know it will take time, but I'm so glad to hear he's starting to relax more."

"Me too," her mom said. Her attention turned toward her buzzing phone on the counter.

When her mom read what was on her phone, Riley noticed her mom's expression changed to one of concern. "Is everything okay, mom?"

Her mom looked up and smiled tightly, "Oh, yes, everything is fine. I just have to make a quick call," she said as she headed to the office where Riley assumed her dad was working.

Riley didn't believe her mom. Something was up. "That was weird," she said to Finn.

"Maybe she found out her hydrangeas aren't going to bloom, and she's calling the landscapers," Finn joked.

Riley chuckled. "No, I don't think that's it." She held her index finger up to her mouth and said, "Shh," as she tiptoed toward her dad's office which sat just off the family room. Finn followed her.

Riley and Finn stood just outside the closed door to the office and could hear her parents talking. Her dad said, "Why don't we just give him a call?"

Riley figured they could be talking about the landscaper, but her mom wouldn't have been secretive or gone behind closed doors with her dad to have a conversation about hydrangeas that weren't going to bloom. It had to be something else, but what?

Riley and Finn heard her mom put the phone on speaker and then ringing. After the third ring, they heard, "Detective Rycroft." Riley jolted her head back from the door and raised her eyebrows at Finn. The best friends looked at one another with wide eyes and they listened.

"Hey, Nick, it's Jack and Priscilla Carson. We have you on speaker."

"Hey, I'm guessing you heard from the Murphys?" Detective Rycroft asked as Riley and Finn faced each other with matching, jaw-dropped faces before turning back to continue listening intently.

"Yes, and this sounds scary," Riley's mom said.

"Well, we don't know if it's related, but I wanted to let you guys know since you have a dog. Too many are turning up missing, and we think there might be more to it, but that's about all I can say right now."

Riley didn't like the sound of that.

"Can I ask how many have gone missing?" Riley's dad asked.

"A total of six," Detective Rycroft said.

Riley felt her stomach tighten.

"Do you think there could be more?" Riley heard her mom ask with fear in her voice.

"We're not really sure. I just want you all to be mindful," Detective Rycroft said.

"Absolutely. We always keep Buster on a leash and of course, the yard is fenced." Riley's dad said.

"Good. I don't want to scare you. I just want you to be aware," Detective Rycroft said. "It could be nothing."

"Are you guys eavesdropping?" Riley spun at the sound of her sister's voice.

"Shh!" Riley headed quietly to the hallway that met the family room. She whispered to her sister, "Mom and dad were just talking to Detective Rycroft. We have to be really careful with Buster because six dogs have gone missing lately."

Hailey smirked, "They probably just got loose. You make everything so dramatic."

"No," Finn said sharply, "she isn't. Detective Rycroft said for us to be mindful. They are afraid it's more than just lost dogs."

Hailey's expression turned to one of concern. "Really?"

Riley nodded, "Yeah, he sounded really serious."

"That's crazy, I wonder what it could be," Hailey said.

"Who knows," Riley said. "Let's just be careful."

CHAPTER EIGHTEEN

Exploring Bulloch Hall

A week had passed since Riley and Finn heard her parents talking to Detective Rycroft, but neither of their parents said anything to them about all those lost dogs. As they rode their bikes to Bulloch Hall for Riley's mom's first tour of the day, Riley said, "What do you think about the lost dogs? It seems weird that our parents haven't said anything to us."

Finn said, "Yeah, I guess it could be that it's not as serious as we thought."

Riley wasn't so sure. "Or maybe our parents don't want to worry us."

"True," Finn said. "Since our dogs are inside dogs and always leashed when we go out, maybe they aren't worried."

Riley thought that sounded reasonable. "Yeah, I guess you're right."

As they turned down Bulloch Avenue, Finn picked up his pace, his eyebrows arched up. "It's so cool that your mom is working at Bulloch Hall. We should see if we can find any tunnel access."

Riley sped up too, a smile grew across her face. "I know! We'll keep an eye out when she's giving us the tour. See if there are any places where there could logically be a tunnel."

They coasted down the street past Mimosa Hall. "Wouldn't it be amazing if we found a tunnel?"

"It would be so cool," Finn said as they entered the gates of Bulloch Hall, turning left to park their bikes in the parking lot. After the kids locked their bikes up on a rack, they headed toward a path between the house and a small white building. Finn said quietly, "If we don't see anything inside, we'll check the grounds when we finish the tour."

Riley surveyed the large landscape. "Yeah, it makes sense to check out here as well, just in case."

Finn stopped at the side of the small white building that had a sign about tours and ticket prices. "Do we need tickets for the tour?"

"My mom already bought some for us. She said to pick them up in the gift shop and text her when we got here." Riley pulled out her phone to send a quick text to her mom; then they headed into the small gift shop where a nice older lady greeted them.

"Welcome, are you here for the tour?" The lady behind the counter asked.

Riley smiled. "Yes, ma'am. I'm Riley Carson. My mom is a new docent here, and she bought two tickets for us and said to pick them up here."

The lady smiled brightly. "How lovely to meet you! We're so excited to have your mom here." The lady pulled two tickets from under the counter and handed them to Riley. She looked at the clock on the wall. "The first tour doesn't start for fifteen minutes. You're welcome to look around here, or, I'm sure your mom wouldn't mind you heading over to the house to see her before the tour starts."

"Thanks," Riley said. She noticed Finn already looking around and joined him.

"There's so much cool stuff in here. Look at these old maps," Finn said. There were copies of old maps of the area that they sold in poster size.

"Cool," Riley said as she looked around. Everything in the shop related to the South. Of course, a lot of the stuff related to the Civil War since the home and area had so much activity during the war. They sold lots of books, mostly historical, some cookbooks, art from local artists, and lots of little gift items. Riley especially liked a watercolor of a cotton plant as it reminded her of her 'Mill Cotton Not Puppies' design. Riley marveled at the plant that looked so interesting and created something so useful. While she enjoyed browsing in the shop, she couldn't wait to get into the house. "Let's go see my mom," she told Finn. "We can come back in here after the tour."

Finn agreed, and they headed out the door they came in through and took the path to the house. The pretty, white house had a simple design but appeared so grand. It had four tall, thick, white columns along the front porch where one could sit in a rocking chair and enjoy the view. They climbed the seven steps up to the porch, and Riley lightly tapped on the old, wooden front door.

"Hey, you two," Her mom said with a bright smile as she opened the large door. "Come on in!"

Riley and Finn stepped into the wide entry hall which had wooden benches on each side and a view to a large staircase that started at the middle of the hallway. Off the entry hall were openings leading to various rooms. The home had a simple decor, but in its day, it would have been very grand and impressive. "Isn't it just beautiful?" Riley's mom asked.

Riley gazed up at the tall ceilings and walked to the first pair of doorways on either side of the entry hall. Her mom said, "That's the parlor on the right and a sitting room on the left. The sitting room has access to the master bedroom, and the parlor opens up to the dining room."

Riley went right, into the parlor. A rope stanchion kept visitors on the left side of the room. "This is so cool. Look at that piano. It's really pretty."

"Yes, this room is really special because it's where guests gathered for the wedding of Mittie Bulloch to Theodore Roosevelt, Senior; they were the parents of our twenty-sixth president, Teddy Roosevelt."

"That's so cool. Presidential history right here in Roswell!" Finn said.

"Yep," Riley's mom said. She moved in between the parlor and dining room. "This is where Mittie and Theodore stood when they took their vows." She looked at her watch. "I know you two want to explore, so have a look around, but don't touch anything or go behind any of the barricades. I'll be in the entry way waiting on other guests.

"Really, mom?"

"Yep, I know you don't have a lot of time, but do a little ghost hunting and get back up here in ten minutes."

"Cool!" Finn said. "Let's start in the cellar."

Riley's mom pointed to the back of the house. "Go past

the staircase, and you'll see another staircase that goes down-stairs. There's really only anything of interest to the right, the cook's kitchen and a root cellar. On the left is a room we use when schools visit, and it's basically empty."

"Great, thanks mom," Riley said as she and Finn scur-ried off to the back of the house.

Once they got downstairs, Finn said, "I'm going to turn my recorder on, just in case, but I really want to see if we can find tunnels."

"Me too," Riley said as they went right to the kitchen and started looking around. The narrow room had brick floors and walls. On the main interior wall stood a large fireplace for cooking and a small brick oven in the wall to the left of the fireplace. What really caught Riley's eye was an open doorway blocked by a small picket fence. You could see into it but couldn't go into the space. A few stairs led to a lower level with a dirt floor. "This is interesting."

Finn joined her at the short fence. "Yeah, this is a pos-sibility." He craned his neck to see to the left. "I can't see all the way around because the door is blocking the left side, but it's a small space." Items that might have been used back when the Bullochs lived here decorated the space so guests could see what the room might have been used for. On the wall opposite the stairs stood an old wooden cabinet con-taining various implements. A bench sat on the right wall, and another in the left corner next to the cabinet. In front of the cabinet, stood a large wooden barrel filled with a bunch of fake vegetables.

"I wish we could see around the door," Riley said. The

door opened into the room, and it blocked most of the left side of the room.

Finn looked at her. "Do you think we can take a quick look?"

Riley didn't like that idea. "My mom told us not to go over any barricades. I don't want to do something she specifically asked us not to do."

Finn nodded. "You're right. That would be wrong of us. Besides, we don't have that much time anyway."

Riley said, "I'm going to take a few pictures so we can reference the space later."

"Cool, then let's take a look in the other room."

When Riley finished taking pictures, they checked out the other room in the cellar. "Your mom was right. This is basically an empty room." Displays hung on the wall about what life was like for kids those days and what kind of toys they played with. A large area rug covered a brick floor.

"Yeah," Riley said. "It looks like this is where they give presentations to young kids." She could hear her mom greeting people upstairs. "Let's go join the tour. Maybe we'll have time later to look around more."

Riley and Finn climbed the narrow staircase with the low ceiling and walked down the hallway toward the front of the house. They saw a handful of people seated on the wooden benches in the entry hallway, waiting for the tour to begin. Riley chuckled and said so only Finn could hear, "I bet we're the only kids who tour this house and aren't on a field trip."

Finn laughed as he surveyed the much older patrons. "Yeah, imagine what Corey would say if he saw us here."

Riley giggled and thought about the last time they saw Corey, and then she had a thought and couldn't believe she hadn't thought of it sooner.

Riley thoroughly enjoyed the tour with her mom, and afterward, as her mom guided the group back to the front door, she told her so. "Mom, that was really interesting! You did a great job."

Her mom put an arm around her shoulders and gave her a squeeze. "Thanks, Roo. I was a little nervous, but they prepared me well, and you know how I love these elegant old homes."

"I liked all the history about the Civil War," Finn said. "The displays upstairs have so much to read. I could spend an hour in each room!"

Riley's mom smiled. "Are you sure you're not trying to get some time in here to search for ghosts?"

"Oh no, we'd need much more than an hour to do that," Finn said making Riley and her mom laugh.

A family approached the porch. Riley's mom said quietly, "It looks like I have my next group, but once I figure out when it's slow, you two can come back and do a little investigating and learning, of course." She winked as she said this.

"That'd be great," Finn said, his eyes sparkled at the thought of finding the tunnels.

"Yeah, mom, thanks," Riley said and gave her a hug. "Have a great day. We really did enjoy the tour."

Riley's mom gave her a kiss on top of her head. "I'm so glad. Make sure to take a look around the grounds. The slave quarters are interesting, and the formal garden is really pretty."

"Will do!" Riley said. "Thanks again, mom!"

As Riley and Finn bounded down the wooden porch steps, Finn said, "Let's definitely look around the grounds to see if there's any sign of a tunnel."

"Absolutely," Riley said as they set off down the gravel path to the rebuilt slave quarters. "It's hard to imagine people used to have slaves, isn't it?" Riley asked. "I think of Mister Oscar and what his life must have been like. Who knows, he may have even worked here on this land."

"Yeah. It sure is crazy that things were like that back then," Finn said as their footsteps crackled on the gravel path.

Riley interrupted, "Oh! I almost forgot."

Finn slowed and turned to look at Riley. "What?"

"Earlier, when you mentioned how Corey would make fun of us for coming on this tour, I had a thought and almost forgot all about it."

"Yeah?"

"Right, so, remember when we saw that old lady and her dog save Corey from that huge snake?"

"Yeah."

"I filmed it."

"Yeah?"

"I have video evidence of a pit bull saving Corey Thornton from a snake!"

Finn thought for a second then it dawned on him. "Oh my gosh! We need to send that video to the city council!"

"I know! If we can show them that these dogs aren't all bad, maybe that will really help us overturn that stupid law."

"That's a great idea," Finn said. "There are so many people lobbying city council about overturning the law. This might give them the best ammunition yet!"

"Especially since Corey's dad is on the city council," Riley added.

As the friends walked up to the slave quarters, Riley had another thought. "Make sure to record while we're out here. You never know what we might catch, and they say on the ghost tour that the ghost of a young slave has been seen running up and down the fence between the house and the slave quarters."

Finn held up his recorder which hung from his neck. "I'm one step ahead of you. I've had it recording since we were in the cellar."

"Cool," Riley said. "You have my mom's entire tour recorded. She might be interested to listen back to it." Riley peered into the small room of one of the slave quarters. "This is tiny. These spaces had to have been crowded."

"And hot."

"Can you imagine?" Riley said. "We take things like air conditioning for granted."

"Totally," Finn said, and he really couldn't say much else.

After looking around the slave quarters, which could only be viewed from the doorway, the kids walked around to a newer event area with a pavilion and pretty outdoor fireplace, but no sign of any tunnels. There was a pond off in the distance, but they didn't think a tunnel would be near a pond or that far from the home. They walked across the front of the home and took a wooden walkway to the formal garden which sat on the opposite side of the house. Riley's mom was right, the formal garden looked beautiful, but unfortunately, there didn't appear to be any tunnel access in it. The garden contained nicely trimmed boxwood hedges, beautiful hydrangea bushes, rose bushes, and all kinds of pretty plants that Riley couldn't have identified without the little signs in front of them. A paved walkway went from one end of the garden to the other and at each end stood a pretty, white, arched trellis.

Finn grew frustrated and let out a heavy breath. "Let's walk around the back of the house and see what we can find."

Riley nodded and they headed back out the way they came, to the side of the house. The red brick foundation appeared old yet undisturbed. When they got to the back of the house, they noticed an old well and a huge, high retaining wall that edged the property.

"Let's take a look near the well," Finn said.

"Okay," Riley said. But, as they got close, her eagerness waned. "Oh my gosh, this wall is high. That's a steep drop off." She could feel tingling in her feet and took two steps back. "Finn, be careful," she pleaded as he walked along the wall.

"Don't worry, I'm fine." He squatted and peered down the wall to check for any signs of a tunnel. "I don't see anything over here. Let me check on the other side of the well." He walked around the well and along the retaining wall on the other side of it.

Riley walked with him but stayed about four feet back from the wall. "Just be careful."

Finn took his time examining the wall, and Riley wished he would hurry up. As she watched him, something caught her eye. "What the…" She looked over her right shoulder to a walkway that led from the front of the house, between the main house and slave quarters, and around to the cellar. "Finn!"

Finn had been squatting and hopped up. "Did you find something?"

"No, but I swear I just saw something," Riley said.

"What was it?"

"I don't know. I swear I saw a shadow come from the side of the house, but nothing is there."

The kids abandoned their search around the well and headed up the pathway along the side of the home. "What did it look like?" Finn asked.

"It was just a shadow. No details or anything, but it moved fast," Riley said. Her heart beat a little faster than normal, and her breathing quickened.

"Was it like an adult-size?"

"No, it was our size," Riley said as she saw Finn's eyes grow wide and his mouth fall open.

"Let's do an EVP session then!"

CHAPTER NINETEEN

Another Thornton?

After their EVP session on the grounds of Bulloch Hall, Riley and Finn rode back to Riley's house to listen to their recordings. As they approached her house a landscaping truck rattled by them. "That's weird," Riley said to Finn.

"What?" Finn asked, following Riley's gaze to the top of the driveway.

"I wonder whose bike that is?"

"Maybe Hailey has a friend over?" Finn suggested.

Riley laughed, "I don't know if any of Hailey's friends ride bikes. They're too cool for that."

Finn said, "I hope we don't get that way when we're her age."

"I don't think we will," Riley said as they climbed the porch steps. "We'll always enjoy fun stuff."

As they walked inside, Buster came over to greet them. His paws made a light clicking on the hardwood floors. Riley scooped him up and gave him kisses. "Hey buddy, how are you?" As if to answer, Buster licked Riley on the tip of her nose. She kissed him back on the top of his head and set him down then made her way to the kitchen and family room. She noticed her sister sat at the kitchen table with someone she didn't recognize.

"Hey," Riley said. "We just took a tour with mom over at Bulloch Hall. She did really well."

Hailey tossed her blond hair over her shoulder and smiled. "Cool," she said but clearly didn't want to have a conversation. "We're working on something for school. This is Adrian."

The boy sitting at the table smiled at Riley and Finn. He had dark hair and pale skin, and Riley noticed that his eyes sparkled when he smiled. "Hi, I'm Adrian Thornton."

Riley and Finn looked at each other. "As in Corey Thornton?" Finn asked.

"And Hadrian?" Riley added, referring to Corey's dad who was also a city council member who had power in their town.

The boy nodded his head, and for a quick moment, Riley saw something in his eyes that she couldn't place. He then smiled and said, "Yep, that's me. I was named after my dad but go by Adrian."

"He's a third," Hailey said proudly. "Hadrian Thornton the third."

Riley noticed that Adrian looked uncomfortable as a shy grin played across his mouth. "So, how do you guys know my family?"

Well, that's a loaded question, Riley thought to herself.

Finn answered, "Corey's in the same grade as us."

"Cool," Adrian said. His voice sounded soft and kind, not at all like Corey's.

"Well, we've got work to do here so..." Hailey meant for

them to move along.

Buster barked at the back door, and Riley said, "Has he been out lately?"

"We had him out earlier," Hailey said as she looked at her watch. "But it's been a while. You should let him out."

Riley walked over to the back door and let Buster out as she and Finn followed behind him. She turned to Finn after closing the door behind them, "Well, I didn't expect that."

"Me neither," Finn agreed. "For what it's worth, he seems nicer than Corey."

"Yeah, he does, but it's kind of weird to have a Thornton in my house, sitting at my kitchen table." Riley watched Buster who had just found a spot to relieve himself. "Good boy!" she said to him as he caught a scent and kept his nose in the grass, following whatever it was he smelled. "Wait a minute!" Riley said urgently as she took her eyes off Buster and looked at her best friend.

"What?"

"Why don't we show Adrian the video of Corey and the dog that saved him from the snake and see if he can show it to his dad? I mean, he seems more reasonable than Corey, right?"

"That's a great idea," Finn said.

Riley turned to Buster, "Come here, Buster." He still sniffed the grass but paused to look up at her. Riley clapped her hands, "Come on, let's go." Buster proceeded to sit down in the grass with his pink tongue hanging out of his mouth and looked as if he was smiling. Riley said to Finn, "I can't blame him for wanting to enjoy the fresh air and sunshine."

"I know," Finn said. "After all those years being stuck in a cage and not being able to decide what to do and where to go, he deserves to be a little stubborn."

Riley smiled at the thought of that. "We'll let him enjoy the sunshine for a bit while we go talk to Adrian. It won't take long."

Riley and Finn headed back inside and interrupted Hailey and Adrian. "Hey," Riley said. "Sorry to bother you, but Adrian, can I show you something?"

Hailey sighed audibly as Adrian stopped typing on his phone, set it down, and said, "Sure, what's up?"

"Well," Riley said, "I don't know how much you're involved with what your dad does on the city council, but we're working really hard to repeal BSL. I think I have something that might help your dad, the mayor, and city council members realize why we're making a mistake by banning certain types of dogs."

"Riley, I don't think Adrian needs to get involved in your *passion projects*." Hailey said those last two words with such derision, as if they were ridiculous issues that no one else cared about, and it made Riley's blood boil.

Before Riley could say anything, Adrian said, "Actually, I do know about that. What do you have that can change their minds?"

Riley pulled her phone from her back pocket. "Finn and I were going to Founder's cemetery and, well, we saw Corey ahead of us…"

Finn cut her off. "We were ghost hunting and were recording video of the area and caught Corey on camera *interacting* with a pit bull behind a fence."

"Let me guess," Adrian said. "Corey was messing with the dog?"

Riley's eyes grew wide. "Uh, yeah, basically."

"But it's what happened as Corey walked away that we want to show you," Finn said, and Riley caught his point. They didn't want to show Adrian the whole video because they were talking about Corey and how he acted so suspicious.

Riley made sure to turn the volume down on her phone and fast-forward the video to the point just before the dog scaled the fence and potentially saved Corey's life. She heard an engine rumble by their house as she walked over to Adrian and handed him her phone after turning the volume back up. "You don't really need volume, but take a look."

Adrian took the phone from Riley and started the video. Riley stood beside him, and hoped that the video would make enough of an impact on him that he would show it to his dad. They watched as the dog scaled the chain link fence, landed on the sidewalk and grabbed Corey's clothing in its teeth, pulling him backwards. Riley could hear Adrian's breath get caught in his throat as the old lady appeared with the garden hoe raised high above her head. When it fell, you could see the snake's body flip into the air several times before landing still. "Oh my gosh," Adrian said.

Riley's heart rate had sped up after watching that again. "Crazy, huh?"

Adrian handed the phone back to Riley, and Finn said, "We took pictures of the dead snake so we could identify it.

It was a copperhead."

"A huge copperhead," Riley said. "And that dog saved Corey from stepping on it."

Adrian's eyes were still wide. "Yeah, send it to me, and I'll show it to my dad."

"Thanks," Riley said. "I'll edit the video to just this part since it's really long. Do you want me to text it?"

"Yeah," Adrian said as he pulled his phone out. "I'll text you so you have my number. What's your number?"

Riley gave Adrian her number. "Thanks so much. I really do think that dog saved Corey, and it might just give the mayor and city council a better perspective of dogs. It's not about their breed. Any dog can be aggressive."

Adrian wore a knowing expression then smiled. "Absolutely."

Riley didn't know if he meant 'you're welcome' or agreed with her last statement. In any case, it made her happy that he would help. "Sorry to bother you guys," she said to Hailey and Adrian. "We're going to grab Buster then listen to some EVPs in the basement."

Riley and Finn headed back outside to get Buster, but he was nowhere to be found.

CHAPTER TWENTY

Gone With The Wind?

Riley started to panic. She and Finn called for Buster, but he wasn't there. Riley looked amongst the bushes and around the perimeter of the yard when Finn called her to the side of the house. The Carson's fence partially enclosed both side yards, and Finn stood by the gate which was open. Riley felt her throat tighten, and she put her hand to her heart. "Oh no!"

Finn said, "This is how I found it. It must have been unlatched." The gate hung open about a foot, plenty of room for Buster to get out.

Riley pushed open the gate and looked for Buster, calling his name as she went with Finn trailing behind her. Riley made her way to the front yard, but still no sign of Buster. She called and called. Finn too. "Maybe he went up to the front door?" Riley said hopefully as she and Finn ran up the porch steps. Unfortunately, he wasn't on the porch. Riley ran inside. "Hailey!" She ran into the kitchen, "Buster's gone!"

Hailey jumped up, "Gone?"

Riley began to cry. "Yes, the back gate is open, and he's nowhere to be found. We have to find him!"

Adrian got up now too. "I'll help. Let's search the neighborhood. He can't be far."

All four kids went out the front door to find Buster. Adrian was right, Riley thought. He couldn't be far. He's small and might still be nearby.

Finn looked at Riley, "Let's go to Hawk's house. Buster loves going over to play with Lennox. Then we'll go to my house in case he's made his way there."

"Can you call your mom?" Riley asked in between tears. "See if she's home and can help us?"

"Yeah," Finn said as he pulled out his phone and called his mom.

Adrian straddled his bike. "Hailey and I can ride around and look for him. That way, we can cover more ground." He looked at Hailey. "Grab your bike."

Hailey looked unsure of what to say. "Um, I don't have a bike."

"Take mine," Riley ordered. "We have to find Buster fast!" Riley didn't stick around to see if Hailey had any trouble with the bike. She and Finn set off across the street to Hawk's house. When they got there, Riley frantically knocked on the door.

Hawk answered quickly with a questioning glance, and Lennox smiled happily beside him. "Hey guys, everything okay?" He searched Riley's face, which she knew must be red and tear-streaked.

"No," she replied. "Buster's gone!" She started to cry more after she said this. It just couldn't be true.

"Oh no," Hawk said. "What happened?"

Finn explained that he found the gate open, and Buster

must have gotten out. "We came here to see if maybe Buster came to visit Lennox. Can we have a look around your yard?"

"Of course," Hawk said. "Let's go." He looked at Lennox. "Sorry buddy, you have to stay here." He closed the front door, and they looked around his yard, calling for Buster. Hawk also had a fenced backyard, so they walked along the perimeter searching for Buster. Unfortunately, there were no signs of the little dog. Hawk looked concerned, and Riley knew that if anyone knew the feeling of losing a dog, it was Hawk. After the city confiscated Lennox, Hawk had trouble coping. "Maybe it'll help if I bring Lennox out to search. Maybe that will help Buster find us? I'll muzzle him up, and we'll start looking."

"Thanks," Riley said gratefully. "We're going to go to Finn's house to see if he might have headed that way."

"Ten-four," Hawk said. "I'll head to the front of the neighborhood then, so we can cover more ground. I have my phone on me. Call me if you find him, and I'll do the same."

"Thanks," Finn said with a weak smile to Hawk and a concerned glance at Riley who already headed down the driveway, frantically calling Buster. He jogged after her and joined her. "Buster! Busterrrr!"

The whole way to the Murphy's house, Riley and Finn called for Buster, and they could faintly hear Adrian and Hailey doing the same thing. As they walked up Finn's street, he said, "My mom texted that she would alert the rescue groups she works with. Then she'll help us look."

This made Riley more nervous. "But, shouldn't he be close? I mean, shouldn't we find him soon?"

"I hope so," Finn said. "My mom just wanted to make sure. Sometimes people pick up a stray and immediately take them to a vet to get scanned for a microchip."

"But he has his collar on," Riley said. "If someone finds him, they can just call us." She thought as she said this. "My mom's number is on his tag. I need to call her!" Riley pulled her phone out of her pocket and called her mom but got voice mail. Frustration crept in as she looked at the time. "She's probably in the middle of a tour." She started to cry again.

Finn said, "I'll call the number for Bulloch Hall and have them get a message to her to call you ASAP." Finn pulled out his phone as they walked up his driveway. After getting the number from their website, he called and left the message. "They're going to have her call as soon as this tour is finished. It's only twenty more minutes. I told them they didn't need to interrupt the tour. Is that okay?"

Riley nodded despondently. "It's not like she can do anything. If someone has him and is waiting to hear back, they will have left a message."

Riley and Finn checked all around his yard, and when his mom saw them out the back window, she joined them. "Oh, Riley, I'm so sorry." She gave Riley a comforting hug that only a mom could give. She rubbed Riley's back and then held her by the shoulders and looked at her earnestly. "We will find him. Don't you worry."

Riley didn't know how she could possibly not worry. The more time passed, the more worried she became. This felt like the time Sammy went missing, but he had been behind

Hawk's house with his collar hung up on a log. She only wished that was the case this time. After searching around Finn's house and street, they found nothing. No one who was out in their yards had seen Buster, but they said they would keep an eye out and be sure to help.

"Why don't we head back to your house, Riley, so we can knock on doors to see if the neighbors have seen him," Finn's mom said.

"That sounds like a good idea," Riley said, still so scared that they hadn't found Buster yet.

"Hop in the car. We'll drive over," Mrs. Murphy directed as they headed to the garage.

Mrs. Murphy drove slowly, and they had the windows down, calling for Buster the whole time. When they got back to her house, Riley, Finn, and his mom went door to door, but no one had seen Buster. Just as she felt herself about to breakdown for the third time today, Riley's phone rang. It was her mom. "Mom, hey," Riley said anxiously.

"Hey sweetie, what's going on? Is everything okay?"

"No," Riley's voice cracked upon hearing her mom's concerned voice, "Buster is missing!" Riley began to sob.

"Oh no! What happened?"

"Finn and I took him outside, but he wasn't ready to go in yet." Riley heaved and sobbed, catching her breath. "He was enjoying the sun, Mom, and we went inside to talk to Hailey. When we went back out, he was gone!" Riley sobbed harder now. "Mom, the gate was left open and he got out. We've been looking everywhere and can't find him!"

"Oh, Roo, I know you are just sick about this, but we'll

find him, just like we found Sammy." Her mom clearly understood how she felt.

"Mom, has anyone called you to say they found him?" Riley asked as she wiped the back of her arm under her nose. "Your number is on his tag. If someone found him, maybe they've called you?"

"Hang on," her mom said, "I do have a couple of missed calls. Let me check."

Riley felt a measure of hope. She said to Finn and his mom, "She has some missed calls, she's checking."

"Oh, I hope someone has found him," Mrs. Murphy said as she clutched her chest.

Just then, Adrian and Hailey rode up the driveway. "Did you find him?" Hailey asked eagerly, searching for signs of their beloved dog.

"No," Finn said. "She's on the phone with your mom, checking to see if anyone called her number from his tag."

Hailey and Adrian shared a pained glance. "What?" Riley said, feeling even more anxious. "What is it?"

Hailey said, "When we rode by the house, Adrian found this in the gutter."

Adrian held up a dog bone-shaped tag, and Riley lost it, crying uncontrollably. Her mom came back on the line, and Riley handed the phone to Mrs. Murphy. Riley was too upset to even form sentences. "It looks like he caught it on something because the circular clasp is stretched out. He might have caught it on something, and it tore off?" Adrian offered as he handed the tag to Riley so she could see for herself. Riley inspected the tag with the name 'Buster' and her mom's phone number engraved on one side and a green heart on the other. It matched his green collar. Riley could see that the circular clasp had been stretched out to the point of almost being straight on one end. She clutched the tag to her heart and cried some more. She couldn't lose Buster, she just couldn't.

CHAPTER TWENTY-ONE

Another Lost Dog

Early the next morning, Riley and her dad drove around and hung flyers that Riley designed the night before. At the top of the flyer in big, block letters it said, 'LOST DOG.' Below that featured a current picture of Buster and his name. Below that, it included her mom's number, the date he went missing, and the name of their neighborhood. 'REWARD' dominated the bottom of the flyer in large, bold print. As they drove, Riley hoped and prayed she would see him. That he was safe and alive, just lost. While Riley and her dad were out driving, her mom and Hailey, with the help of Finn and his parents, canvassed the neighborhood again, hung signs, and knocked on doors. They visited every home in their small neighborhood, but still, no one had seen him. Of course, all of the neighbors promised to keep an eye out.

Riley and her dad arrived home tired. Riley was still so scared. Her mom asked, "How far did you get?"

Riley's dad took a seat at the kitchen table and gratefully accepted a mug of coffee from his wife. "We posted signs all up and down Mimosa, Coleman, and Willeo including the neighborhoods off those streets."

Riley drank from a glass of orange juice her mom gave

her and added, "We also hung them around the square, but none of the businesses were open yet. So we'll have to go back."

Riley's mom sat down with them. "It's probably a good idea to go to all the businesses along Canton Street too."

Riley agreed. "Yeah, we can go down there once they open." Her phone buzzed on the table. "Eve said she and Evan are posting flyers in their neighborhood. Did they come pick some up?"

Her mom smiled. "They did. You have such good friends, Roo. They really want to help us find Buster."

Riley felt a lump in her throat and fought back tears yet again. Her dad seemed to notice and grabbed her hand. "Don't worry, Roo. We'll find him."

"But dad," Riley cried, "there are so many dogs missing right now. What if someone stole him? What if he gets hit by a car?" The tears started to flow quickly as she thought of all the scenarios that could have happened. "If he were close, we would have found him. Either...either something happened, and he's hurt...or worse, he's been taken. You know how popular Yorkies are." She sobbed uncontrollably now. "And it's all my fault!"

Riley's dad got up and put his arms around her, trying to comfort her in some small way. "Roo, it's not your fault that the gate wasn't closed all the way. You didn't mean for him to get out."

"Yeah," Riley cried, "but I should have stayed out there with him and watched him. Instead I went inside, so concerned with telling Adrian about the dog that saved Corey, that I wasn't there for *my* dog." Riley now hugged her dad back and sobbed into his shoulder. This felt like déjà vu. At least when Sammy went missing, he had been found quickly. She had a feeling that they wouldn't be so lucky this time.

Riley's phone buzzed again and she quickly checked it. "Finn's on his way over."

Riley's mom said, "Finn and his parents were a great help. While you two were out, we went to every single house in the neighborhood and gave everyone a flyer. All the neighbors here know to be on the lookout, and we've put signs on every single sign post in our neighborhood. Everyone said they will keep an eye out for Buster."

Riley knew her mom tried to reassure her, but she didn't feel like anything could make her feel better, anything except finding Buster.

As if her mom could feel her energy, she laid a delicate hand on Riley's wrist and said, "Hey." Riley looked up at her mom with sad blue eyes. "We're going to find him. Your dad and I are going to call vets offices and shelters to make sure they know he's missing, and we'll keep calling them regularly. I'll even go there with flyers myself so they know we're just waiting to take him home."

Now Riley's dad chimed in. "Your mom is right. Mrs. Murphy said that shelters and animal control offices are so busy that often it's best to go in person. We will take care of that, and I want you to monitor shelters online to see if he pops up there."

Riley nodded. She felt better that her parents were as invested in working to find Buster as she was. "I'll keep checking everywhere online; neighborhood sites, social media, shelters, everything. I'm sure Finn will too."

Her parents smiled at her. Her dad got up and said, "I know you're probably not hungry, Roo, but let me fix us some breakfast."

"Thanks, dad," Riley said with a weak smile. She said a silent prayer that Buster would be found safely.

When Finn got to Riley's house, he joined Riley at the kitchen table while her dad finished cooking. "So, my mom contacted Angels and several other rescue groups. She forwarded them your digital flyer, and they are all posting on their social media. Plus, my mom is going to do some digital canvassing and spread the word online - in groups and on pages. She's going to make sure everyone knows we're looking for Buster."

Riley's mouth turned up in a faint smile of appreciation. "That's so nice of her, thanks."

"Ri, don't worry, we'll find him," Finn said, and he actually sounded confident with his words. "I talked to Eve. She and Evan are going to come over around noon so we can hand out flyers along Canton Street. We'll ask businesses to post signs, and it's a nice day so there should be a lot of people out shopping, eating on the sidewalks...We'll pass out flyers to everyone we see!"

Riley appreciated Finn's optimism and it really did help her change her mindset. "Thanks so much, Finn," she said. This time her smile brightened.

Her mom said, "Since you've got some time before they get here, I'm going to get more flyers printed." She looked at the clock. "I shouldn't be more than a half hour, and that still gives us plenty of time." With that Riley watched as her mom grabbed her purse and headed to the garage.

"Here sweetheart," her dad said as he put a plate of French toast in front of her. "Your favorite."

"Thanks, dad," she said gratefully as her stomach growled.

"I made some for you, too, Finn. I wasn't sure if you had eaten yet."

Finn smiled. "Thanks, Mister Carson. I always have room for more breakfast."

When the three of them finished eating, Riley and Finn offered to clean up so Riley's dad could go make some phone calls about Buster. Riley thought it was a little odd that he closed his office door, but figured her dad didn't want her to get upset again. "Thanks for all your help, Finn. I really appreciate it," Riley said as she washed the pan her dad had used to cook their breakfast.

Finn stood by with a towel. "No problem. I know you would do it for me too."

Riley handed Finn the pan. "I hope this ends well like it did when Sammy went missing. I just keep thinking about the phone call we overheard between my parents and Detective Rycroft."

Finn dried the pan and thought back to that day when they stood outside Mr. Carson's home office and eavesdropped on the conversation with Eve's dad. "He said there were six dogs missing and to be careful, right? That he thought there might be more to it?"

Riley searched her memory too. "Yeah, he said we should be vigilant. If it's just lost dogs, then why would we need to be vigilant? There's got to be more to it."

Finn agreed as he handed Riley the dry pan to put away. "Detective Rycroft must be onto something, and I think we need to find out what that is."

Riley felt renewed hope. If they could find out what Detective Rycroft thought might be going on, maybe they could find Buster!

CHAPTER TWENTY-TWO

Canvassing Canton Street

Riley, Finn, Eve, Evan, and Tim Harrington took to Canton Street to hand out flyers to businesses and everyone out and about enjoying this beautiful May day. Evan dropped Eve and Tim off on the north end of Canton Street, close to Woodstock Road, so they could cover one side of the street. Next, Evan drove Riley and Finn to the south end of Canton Street where they started canvassing at Heart of Roswell Park.

Even though Riley normally felt shy around strangers, she was bold today. She talked to everyone who crossed her path about Buster and handed out flyers while Finn or Evan went into the businesses to ask them to hang signs.

As they walked past the funky clothing store, Gifted, Evan said, "Everyone has been so nice and agreed to post at least one sign in their front window. Some even said they would also post at their host stand or cash register too."

"I'm so glad," Riley said. "We need everyone to know that Buster is gone, and that we're offering a reward." She looked at Finn and fidgeted with her key necklace. "Do you think someone might have stolen him to try to get reward money?"

Finn thought for a moment. "Well, that's an idea. I have heard that people will do that..."

"That's horrible," Evan said. "I can't believe people actually do that."

"They do that and worse," Finn said, then caught himself. He looked at Riley, "I'm sorry."

Riley sighed. "Don't worry. It's not like I haven't already thought of every worst-case scenario. I would almost rather someone take him to get the reward money than to take him and keep him." She choked up when she said this and willed herself not to get worked up again. She breathed deeply to steady herself.

After recalling the conversation they had overheard between Detective Rycroft and Riley's parents, Finn had an idea. "A lot of dogs have gone missing lately. Evan, any idea if your dad has any theories?"

Evan looked at Finn and brushed his dark hair out of his eye. "Nah, my dad doesn't talk about cases. He's definitely been working a lot lately." He seemed to think about it. "He's been working even when he's home, but I'm not sure what case he's working on."

Riley and Finn exchanged a knowing glance. They knew he warned Riley's parents to be vigilant, but was it because he worked on the case, or perhaps, he had just heard about things at the precinct and wanted to warn his friends? Either way, Riley felt intrigued and hopeful.

###

When they got to The Downtown Pooch, Riley started to get emotional. "If I go in there and see Sam or Marina, I'm going to cry."

Evan didn't hesitate. "Don't worry, I've got this." He bounded up the steps two at a time and opened the pretty front door with flyers in hand.

Finn said, "I can go inside and talk to the customers if you want to stay out here."

Riley smiled and nodded. "Thanks," she said quietly. "There are plenty of people walking around, so I'll stay out front." She knew it was silly, but Sam and Marina knew Buster and his story. Buster loved coming to The Downtown Pooch to get treats and see the shop owner and her employee. They loved him, and he loved them. Sam kindly allowed Riley to spend as much time as she wanted training Buster in and around her shop. They truly cared about dogs at The Pooch, as Riley liked to call it.

As expected, a lot of people were walking past the shop and Riley talked to several groups of people about Buster. A few recognized her from the BSL case and sympathized with her at her loss, encouraging her that she would find her beloved dog. The one thing Riley constantly found when it came to dog lovers was they truly understood the bond humans have with their dogs. Some people think a dog is just a dog, but true dog lovers know how amazing these creatures are and what a part of the family they become.

When Finn and Evan came out of the store, Riley had probably talked to six groups of people. "So," Finn said hesitantly, "Sam said she hoped to see us here for Alive in

Roswell this week with the anti-BSL group."

Riley thought for a moment. "Oh, that's right. That's this Thursday," Riley said. She breathed in deeply then exhaled. "I hope we'll have found Buster by then, but if not, it will be a good opportunity to hand out more flyers."

Finn nodded solemnly. "I was thinking the same thing."

An old, white home sat next to The Downtown Pooch just across from the driveway leading to the shop's parking lot. In the yard of this home, one of the rare homes on the street that was still an actual home, not a business, Riley spotted a short, stout man with white hair. He had a cane and tried to pick up an orange cone that fell on its side in his yard. Riley jogged up to help. "Let me help you with that!"

The old man stood from a bent-over position and smiled. "Thank you," he said with a gruff tone to his voice. "Someone must have thrown this in my yard. I use it to put at the end of my driveway so people don't block it."

At this point, Finn and Evan joined Riley. "Where would you like us to put it?" Riley asked because she couldn't make out an actual driveway.

The old man pointed a pudgy finger toward a patch of gravel along the side of his yard adjacent to the asphalt of the parking lot. "Right in the middle of that gravel. That's my driveway, and I don't want people blocking it. They're always blocking it!"

Evan smiled at the man. "We'll take care of it for you."

Riley set the cone in place and looked back at the man. "Right here?" She smiled at him.

"Yes, thank you," the old man said. "If there's an emergency, my driveway can't be blocked."

"Yes, sir," Finn said. He handed the old man a flyer. "Riley's dog went missing out of her yard off Mimosa Street. Will you keep an eye out?"

The old man took the flyer and gave it a hard look. He looked at Riley. "This is your dog?"

"Yes, sir," Riley said.

The old man gave her a slight smile. "I sure will keep an eye out. Mostly around here it's stray cats on account of all the restaurants, but I'll keep an eye out for your dog."

"Thank you so much," Riley said. "I really appreciate it."

"Thank you for helping me out," he said to Riley and her friends. He then turned around and slowly made his way back to his porch.

"I thought he was going to be mean at first," Finn said.

"Yeah, me too," Riley said. "He's probably just old and lonely."

"It was nice of you to help him," Evan said softly.

Riley knew now more than ever how good it felt when you got help when you needed it, and she was happy to pay it forward. "The new ice cream shop is next door. That should be really busy right now," Riley said as they walked along the sidewalk to the business on the other side of the old man's house. She was grateful for the help from her friends and silently prayed that Buster would be found in good shape and soon.

CHAPTER TWENTY-THREE

A Little Help from a Friend

Normally, the last week of school made Riley extremely excited, however, as she trudged through the last Monday of sixth grade, she didn't feel excited. She felt sad and numb. Buster had not been found, and thoughts of her sweet dog and possibilities of his current whereabouts and condition filled her head. Where could he be? Was he scared, hungry, hurt? Was he...still alive? Right now, the extra time to search for Buster served as the best thing about being out of school for summer. As she met Finn to walk home from school, he approached her with a grin on his face. "What's up?" she asked solemnly.

"I know it's not the news you're looking for right now, but I have some good news."

"Oh, yeah?" she said as she kept walking away from school and toward home.

"Yeah. The city council saw your video of Corey and the dog," Finn said, his voice sped up as he spoke. "They're going to meet tomorrow night to revisit BSL."

Riley smiled weakly. "That's great."

"Ri, I know this isn't news that Buster is okay, but this is huge, and you had a lot to do with this. You should be proud," Finn said, and she could tell he tried to hide the irritation he felt.

"I'm sorry, Finn," she said and forced a smile. "This is really good news, and it will hopefully help a lot of dogs and their owners. I'm sorry I can't be more excited."

She could tell Finn felt bad. "I'm sorry, Riley. I can't expect you to push your sadness aside because of this. You've just worked so hard for this to happen, and I'm sorry you can't enjoy it."

Riley didn't know what to say. Finn was right, she couldn't enjoy it because she had a hole in her heart that appeared when Buster disappeared. That poor dog had been through so much, having been raised in an illegal puppy mill, and now missing, she felt so scared for his safety. If only she had stayed in the yard with him.

As they walked home, Riley saw all the signs that she and her friends and family had posted. She called for Buster, and Finn did too. He really was such a good friend.

"Hey, what do you say we listen to the EVP session we recorded at Bulloch Hall?" Finn asked, hopeful that a distraction would help Riley.

Riley knew what Finn was up to but thought it was a good idea. "Only if we can go to your house," she said. "I miss Buster when I'm at home."

Finn smiled, seemingly glad she agreed. "Of course!"

When they got to Finn's house, Molly greeted them the moment they walked in the door. The three of them went to the basement to listen to their recordings. Molly loved Finn, but today, she stuck to Riley like glue. Riley sat on the floor with her back on the sofa, and Molly rested her head in Riley's lap. As Riley gently stroked the top of Molly's head, she said, "I think she knows I'm sad." With that, Molly let out an audible exhale.

Finn busily tapped and clicked away at his laptop but paused and looked at Riley and Molly which made him smile. "She's such a good girl. I'm sure she knows you're sad."

Riley continued to stroke Molly's head, and it made her feel better. "While you're listening to see if we caught anything," she said, "I'm going to search for dogs online. Maybe someone is trying to sell Buster, or maybe he's been spotted in another state. Thank goodness for the internet. I don't know what people did before."

"Okay," Finn said. "Make sure to check the site the rescue groups use when they are trying to adopt out dogs. You never know."

"Yep, I've been stalking that page," Riley said. "Searching for male Yorkies of any age anywhere in the country."

After about fifteen minutes, it appeared Finn found something. He sat up straight and yanked off his headphones. "Got something?" Riley asked as she scrolled through page after page of dogs.

Finn's eyes were wide as he nodded his head. "I think it's Mister Oscar!"

Riley jumped up and sat on the sofa next to Finn. Molly startled and hopped up too, looking at Riley and Finn for reassurance. "Sorry, Molly," Riley said as she stroked Molly on her neck. "It's okay." She looked at Finn and said, "Are you sure?"

Finn nodded. "It sounds just like him." His eyes still wide as he handed Riley the headphones, then cued the recording back up.

Riley listened as she heard herself and Finn talking on the recording. She recalled their location - behind Bulloch Hall when Riley thought she saw something. She heard a man's voice, and it definitely sounded like the familiar voice of Mister Oscar. "Be careful, chil'. They're up ta no good." Riley slipped the headphones off and looked at Finn, her eyebrows raised and eyes bright. "He's talking to me. It's definitely Mister Oscar!"

The friends did their routine, and each wrote down the words they heard so they didn't influence the other. They both wrote the same thing.

Finn nodded. "He's telling you to be careful again. But who is up to no good?"

Riley shook her head. "I have no idea. I wish he had been more specific." She handed Finn the headphones.

"I'll keep listening. See if he says anything else." Finn put the headphones back on and continued to listen to their recording.

Riley remained on the sofa and grabbed her laptop off the coffee table. She continued to look for Buster online, saying her thousandth prayer that he was safe and that she would find him soon.

After about ten minutes, Finn grew excited again. "There's something else! Here, you've gotta hear this!" He handed Riley the headphones which she quickly put over her ears.

Riley closed her eyes because it seemed to help her hear better. She concentrated on the sounds coming out of the headphones. Again, Riley heard her own voice and Finn's, and then very softly in the background, in almost a whisper, she heard Mister Oscar again. Riley's mouth fell open as she slipped the headphones off. She grabbed her paper and pen and wrote what she heard while Finn did the same. They showed each other their paper and again, their statements matched. *The answer is underfoot.*

"We need to figure out who they are," Finn said. "He clearly said *they* are up to no good."

"Yeah, and what answer is underfoot?" Riley was confused about this last sentence. "Whatever it is, it doesn't sound good." For the moment, Riley's sadness and despair over losing Buster disappeared. Mister Oscar used his energy to communicate with them, so she knew it must be important, but she had no idea what he was trying to tell them.

CHAPTER TWENTY-FOUR

An Inside Job?

As Riley and Finn walked home from school on Tuesday afternoon, the topic of what Mister Oscar said to them when they explored Bulloch Hall dominated the conversation. "I can't believe he was there," Riley said. "Do you think he worked there?"

Finn shrugged his shoulders. "I have no idea, but it's cool that he's still hanging around. I wish we could figure out what he meant though."

"I know," Riley agreed. "It's too bad we have our last exams tomorrow, otherwise, we could go back and do another EVP session."

"Yeah, but at least we captured it outside, so we can go by at any time," Finn said as his phone buzzed in his pocket. He pulled it out and tapped the screen and read the message. "It's my mom. She said the city council is voting tonight on whether or not to overturn BSL!"

Riley felt a jolt of excitement and hope. "Tonight? Wow! That would be amazing if they did!"

Finn read the next message that appeared. "She says they aren't taking any more public comments. Just that they will vote tonight."

"Honestly, I don't know what more we can say or do, you know?"

"Yeah," Finn agreed, "there have been so many people working on this, picketing, and generally informing the public. They're probably tired of it."

Riley smiled slightly. "Hopefully, we wore them down. It would be nice for something good to happen."

Finn knew Riley missed Buster badly. He stopped and looked her in the eyes. "Ri, I'm so sorry. I wish there was more I could do to help."

Riley's eyes began to glisten with tears. She turned away from Finn and continued walking. He followed. "I just don't know what else to do. If someone turned him into a vet, shelter, or rescue group, they would scan him for a microchip, and they would contact us. That hasn't happened yet."

Finn drew in a deep breath. "I know, but maybe someone found him and hasn't taken him to a vet yet. When they do, they will scan him."

"I don't know, Finn. That seems kind of like a long shot," Riley fidgeted with the strap on her backpack now. "Since his tag came off, if someone finds him and doesn't see our signs, they won't know we're looking for him. They might keep him." When she said this, her voice caught in her throat. Finn put a hand on her shoulder. She choked, "Or, he might have gotten hit by a car and killed, and since he doesn't have a tag, he won't be identified."

Finn quieted for a moment. "If something bad like that did happen, though, someone should have at least contacted animal control, and they still would have scanned the body.

I know there's probably a million scenarios running through your head, and I'm sorry. I wish you could turn that worry off."

"I really try," Riley said as she wiped a tear off her cheek. "But he went missing on my watch, and I feel horrible about it."

"Ri, it could have just as easily been Hailey, or me...or even Adrian. Anyone could have let Buster out that day. It just happened to be you. I was there too; it could be just as much my fault."

"Adrian," Riley said as she stopped and looked at Finn, the gears turned behind her eyes.

"Yeah, what about him?"

Riley's eyes grew wide. "What if Adrian is just as bad as Corey and opened our gate? What if he had someone come and take Buster?"

Finn looked at Riley doubtfully. "Come on, you really think he'd do something like that? He seems a lot cooler than Corey. Like you'd never guess they were brothers."

"Think about it," Riley said as she became more animated. "Corey doesn't like me, we uncovered the illegal puppy mill that got Mr. Thornton's caretaker in trouble, and I've been making things really difficult for the city council regarding BSL...Mr. Thornton is *on* the council."

Finn still wasn't convinced. "But what would Adrian have to gain out of it?"

"Family loyalty?" Riley suggested.

"I don't know, Ri. He didn't strike me as being like Corey. At all."

Riley playfully slapped Finn on the bicep. "The tag! Adrian found Buster's tag in the street. How convenient is that?"

"But he was inside with Hailey when all this happened." Finn cocked his head and gave Riley a questioning glance.

"Which is a good alibi," Riley said, her words speeding to catch up with her thoughts. "If he worked with someone, they would have planned it that way. And, they would have planned for him to *find*," she used air quotes when she said this last word, "the tag when he was with someone."

Finn chuckled and shook his head. "This would make for a great mystery novel, but I think this is really a stretch, Ri."

Riley sighed with frustration. "I'm not joking," she said as she kicked a pine cone on the sidewalk with force. "You can think this is crazy or far-fetched, but I think this is a very good theory." She picked up her pace, frustrated that her best friend thought she was being unreasonable.

Finn jogged to catch up. "Hey, I'm sorry," he said, and Riley stopped to look at him, sincerity evident in his eyes. "How are you going to test this theory? How will you find out if you're right or not?"

Riley grew pensive. "I don't know, but I'll come up with a plan." She turned on her heel and marched down the side-walk with renewed purpose. Again, Finn picked up his pace to catch up to her.

When she got home, Riley grabbed a snack and went straight to her room to study, even though her mind swirled with thoughts about the possibility of Adrian having something to do with Buster's disappearance. Am I crazy? she thought to herself. Was Adrian like his little brother? Or, is he as different from Corey as I am from Hailey? She knew she had to study and had a sense of relief that her last exam turned out to be a subject she excelled in--social studies. She forced herself to put her wild imagination aside so she could get her studying done before dinner. When she sat down to eat with her family, she would ask Hailey about that dreadful day.

Riley reviewed her social studies notes for almost three hours when her mom called her for dinner. She felt very confident that she knew the material but would have one of her parents quiz her after dinner to be sure. As her family passed each other food and filled their plates, Riley nonchalantly asked her sister about Adrian. "So, Hailey, how long have you and Adrian Thornton been friends?" When she asked this, she noticed her dad look up and lean forward slightly.

"I wouldn't say we're friends," Hailey said as she put a spoonful of broccoli on her plate. "We have a class together and got paired up for a project."

Riley noticed her dad relaxed and sat back in his chair as she said, "If he's anything like his little brother, I don't think you'd want to be friends with him."

"Now Riley," her mom said as she set down a bowl.

"Seriously, mom, Corey is mean," Riley said as she speared a piece of broccoli with her fork.

"You know it's probably because he likes you," Riley's mom said as she cut her food.

"Mom, don't start with that again. Corey definitely doesn't like me. He's my nemesis." Riley got frustrated and had to direct the conversation back to Adrian. She looked at Hailey. "Do you know Adrian well?" As soon as Riley said this, she wished she had worded it better.

Hailey looked guarded. "Um, what are you getting at Riley?"

Riley played it cool and dipped her spoon into her mashed potatoes. "I've just never seen him around and wondered if he's anything like his bully brother."

This seemed to make sense to Hailey, and her demeanor softened. "He's definitely not a bully. He's quiet and kind of a loner at school. You'd think he'd be more popular since he's Hadrian Thornton's son, but he's not. He keeps to himself."

Their mom wore a goofy grin as she said, "He sure is cute. Is there anything going on between you two?"

Hailey blushed, "Mom!"

"Well, he comes from a notable family," she said and seemed pleased with herself. Riley noticed her dad didn't appear to feel the same way as his posture stiffened and concern wrinkled in his brow.

Riley tried to figure out a way to get more information out of her ever-private sister. "It was nice of him to help us look for Buster. I don't think Corey would have done that."

"I thought so too," Hailey said. "But, honestly, what was he going to do? Stay here while we all went searching?"

"Well, I guess he could have just gone home," Riley

suggested. She tried to figure out how to word this next question. "When you let Buster out earlier, did you happen to notice the gate?"

"No, I never go around the side to check to see if the gate is open. I just assume it's closed."

Riley nodded in understanding, "Yeah, me too."

Their dad said, "I'm going to get padlocks with a combination so this doesn't happen again. We'll just have to make sure to take them off the gates for the landscapers, then put them right back on."

"That's a great idea, Jack," Riley's mom said before taking a sip of sparkling water.

Riley wanted to continue her line of questioning. "Hailey, when you were out with Buster earlier that day, was Adrian with you?"

"Yeah," Hailey said casually. "We took Buster out before we got started. Why?"

"And you guys stayed in the backyard. You didn't go in or out of the gate?"

"What is this, 20 Questions?" Hailey said as she glared at Riley.

"I'm just trying to go back and figure out what could have happened. How the gate was left open."

"If you're insinuating that I had something to do with this, then you are crazy." Hailey's forked clanged onto her plate. "You and Finn were the ones outside with Buster before he went missing. *You* were the one who left him outside so you could show Adrian that stupid video of his brother getting saved by a dog so you could try to convince his dad to overturn that law."

Riley felt her blood pressure rise. She could hear her heart pounding in her ears as her dad said, "That's enough! This was an accident, and I'm not going to listen to you two go at each other when we're all upset about what happened."

Riley breathed rapidly. Her dad never raised his voice, and she felt bad about how this escalated. She didn't want Hailey to think she blamed her, but she couldn't let her family know her suspicions about Adrian either. "Hailey, I'm sorry. I didn't mean to imply that you had done anything wrong."

Hailey looked surprised and let out a long breath. "I'm sorry too. I know you would never do anything to put Buster in danger, or any dog for that matter."

Just then, Riley's phone rang from the basket on the island. It was the ring tone she had set for Finn's calls, so she hopped up, glad for the interruption. "No ma'am," her mom said. "We're still eating." Riley could tell that her mom meant business so she slowly sat back down.

When Riley's phone stopped ringing, her mom's phone started ringing. Her mom glanced over at the counter where her phone sat. "Mom," Riley pleaded, "what if it's about Buster?"

With that, Riley's mom stood and grabbed her phone on the last ring. "Hello Finn, is everything okay?"

Riley searched her mom's face for information. Had someone found Buster? Was he okay? Her heart rate sped up again. Riley noticed that her mom's expression softened, but it wasn't the reaction she hoped for. If Buster had been found, her mom would be way more excited. She smiled and said, "I'll hand the phone to Riley. She'll want to hear this from you."

Riley looked at her mom's face still trying to place what was going on. "Buster?" she whispered as her heart pounded.

Her mom shook her head, "No, but it's good news."

Riley's hands trembled as she took her mom's phone. "Finn, what's up?"

"Great news!" Finn said through the phone, and Riley could picture the smile on his face. "The city council reversed the BSL law. We don't know if it's because of the video, or all our protesting and educating, but they are reversing it. Pit bulls and their families can go back to life as normal in Roswell."

Riley realized she had been holding her breath and let out a long exhale and smiled. "That's great news, Finn." She meant it and knew she should be proud of this accomplishment. While she still had a hole in her heart with Buster gone, she felt happy for all the other families and dogs who had been dealing with so much stress and uncertainty.

Finn continued, "We're going to celebrate at The Downtown Pooch on Thursday at Alive in Roswell. I'm sure we'll see so many families and supporters out now that their dogs can be out on the streets without muzzles."

Riley genuinely felt happy. She knew she would be even more excited with Buster safe at home, but this really was a great accomplishment. She hoped that Buster's story would have a happy ending like this too, but as more time passed, she grew even more worried that she would never see him again. Riley felt helpless, and the only thing she could do was to continue to put Buster's image out there and pray. She needed a miracle.

CHAPTER TWENTY-FIVE

Something to Celebrate

Not only was Thursday the last day of school, but it was also Alive in Roswell and the gathering to celebrate the reversal of the law that Roswell passed banning pit bulls and pit bull-type dogs. Riley still hadn't heard any news about Buster, and she missed him terribly. She tried to put on a positive attitude and dressed in her 'No Hate, Don't Discriminate' t-shirt, jeans, and sneakers. Tonight would relieve her mind of her constant worries about Buster. Of course, it also presented a great opportunity for her to pass out flyers about Buster, and she planned to take a huge stack with her.

When Riley and Finn arrived at The Downtown Pooch to help set up, a definite party vibe filled the air. The owner, Sam, and her employee, Marina, tied balloons to the front porch and railings along the stairway, and a sign out front announced free doggie ice cream to celebrate BSL being overturned.

"Wow!" Riley said to Sam who tied one last balloon to the porch railing. "This looks amazing."

Sam turned with a big smile on her face. "Hey guys! We definitely have something to celebrate tonight."

Riley couldn't help but smile back, then her smile faded

slightly. "So, I brought more flyers about Buster. Can you set a stack out and let people know when they check out?"

Now Sam's smiled softened. "Of course. Marina's inside. Tell her I said it's okay to make space on the counter."

"Thanks, Sam," Riley said, then headed in the front door.

Once inside, Marina greeted her with a hug. "Congratulations! Your hard work paid off," she said with her pretty German accent.

Riley smiled bashfully. "Thanks, Marina, but it was a team effort. So many people worked so hard to get this done."

"I know," Marina said proudly, "but you started this movement, and you should be very proud."

"That's what I keep telling her," Finn said.

"I'd be happier if he was here to celebrate with us," Riley said showing her stack of flyers to Marina. "Sam said it's okay to put a stack at the counter to give to people when they check out."

Marina looked at Riley as only a mother could. Her shoulders softened, and she took some flyers from Riley. "Of course. I will tell every single person who comes in here about Buster."

Riley looked at the counter, and the front of it had more Lost Dog flyers than it had before. It felt like a punch to the gut. "Marina, all of these dogs are missing?"

Marina inhaled sharply. "I'm afraid so. I just don't know what's going on." Her brow wrinkled as concern washed over her eyes.

Finn looked at Riley, and they shared a knowing look. Something strange was going on.

"How did they go missing?" Finn asked tentatively.

"All different ways," Marina said matter-of-factly. "One woman takes her dog everywhere and left it in the car with the car running to keep the dog cool, and it was stolen from her car. The car wasn't stolen. Nothing was stolen but the dog."

"That's crazy!" Finn said.

Riley scanned the flyers, grateful that Buster's face stood out front and center. "Which one was that?"

Marina came around the counter and pointed at a picture of a handsome French bulldog. "This one. His owner is just devastated."

Riley nodded, completely understanding how the dog's family must feel. Her gaze fixed on the flyers, trying to find a commonality between all the dogs. Amongst the flyers of dogs included two of missing cats.

Finn asked, "Do you think they are all being stolen? Most of these are popular breeds that someone might re-sell for a profit."

Riley's heart sank. If someone stole Buster to sell him for a profit, she may never find him. "I've gotta get some air," she said as she quickly walked out the front door and down the porch steps. She busied herself with the table that Sam had set up for them on the front lawn.

Finn came out after her. "Ri, I'm so sorry. I wasn't thinking. I shouldn't have been having that conversation in front of you."

Riley wiped a tear from her eye and forced a smile. "It's okay. We're doing all we can, and I still want to look into

Adrian some more. I know you think I'm crazy, but I have to follow that hunch."

Finn smiled kindly. "I don't think you're crazy. I understand that you want to follow that through to see if it leads anywhere. I mean, I thought about it, and while I didn't get a weird vibe from Adrian, we have to look at all the evidence and see where it leads us. If there's nothing there, then we move on."

Riley smiled genuinely this time. "You're such a great friend, Finn. Let's enjoy this night. It'll be a great chance to hand out a ton of flyers about Buster, and maybe that will get us a new lead."

Riley had hardly any time to be sad. When she wasn't talking to excited pit bull parents and meeting their precious pups, she handed out flyers and told people about Buster. The doggie ice cream social was first come, first served, and it sold out in the first hour of the event. She had just finished loving on a sweet pair of pibbles (a term of endearment for pit bulls) named Knight and Aston, when she looked up to see another sweet face. It was so great seeing him outside without a muzzle. "Lennox!" Riley said as she hopped up to greet him and Hawk. "I'm so glad y'all made it." She saw a smile appear underneath Hawk's beard. In fact, his smile grew so large that he even showed his white teeth. Riley couldn't help but give him a great big bear hug.

Hawk laughed and when Riley stepped back, he said,

"We wouldn't have missed it for the world." He gave Lennox a loving scratch behind his ears as Riley squatted to pet the sweet dog. "We would have been here earlier if I hadn't gotten tied up with work." He looked around at all the people gathered in the front lawn of The Downtown Pooch. "This is amazing."

"Yeah," Riley said as she stood up and looked at the crowd, "with all these pitties, you guys could create your own group." There were all kinds of dogs out during Alive in Roswell, but tonight, the pit bulls dominated and smiles beamed from faces all over the place.

"You should be so proud," Hawk said.

Riley felt her cheeks flush. "It wasn't just me, there are a whole lot of people who worked hard to overturn that stupid law, and I'm so glad we did it." She squatted down again to scratch Lennox on his chest. "It's so good to see him out without his muzzle. He seems to be enjoying it." The black pit mix did indeed seem to be smiling.

Hawk admired his service dog. "Yeah, I think he's really happy. You might not have done all this on your own, but you sure did save this guy's life and brought a lot of attention to this issue. We're forever grateful."

Riley knew Hawk meant it, especially since he was usually a man of few words. She smiled. "Thank you." She thought perhaps Lennox helped Hawk more than she realized. He seemed much happier and at ease, even being in a crowd. "If only everyone realized how precious dogs are and how much better they make our lives."

"Ain't that the truth?" Hawk said.

As Hawk and Riley surveyed all the beautiful dogs out to celebrate, Finn ran up to them. "Hey Hawk!" Clearly, Finn had something important to say because he quickly looked at Riley and said, "Ri, uh, can you come with me for a second? I have something to show you."

Riley and Hawk looked at each other, and Hawk laughed. "Sounds important. You'd better go have a look," he said to Riley.

"Yeah, uh, okay." Riley didn't know what Finn was up to. "See ya, Hawk. Thanks for coming." With that Riley followed her best friend up the porch steps and into The Downtown Pooch. "What's up," she asked Finn.

Finn's eyes sparkled, and he whispered, "Baby Girl is here."

"What?" Riley asked quietly as she scanned the small store. Since the building used to be a house, you couldn't see much from where they were in the front room. A narrow hallway led to other rooms, and that's the way they headed. "On such a crowded night, that's a good thing. She must really be getting better about being around people and dogs."

"Yeah, she must be," Finn said. "Emily is here with her, and I knew you'd want to see her."

As they turned the corner, they saw Baby Girl and Emily, both seemed to recognize them right away. "Hey there!" Emily said as Baby Girl pulled at her leash to see Riley.

"Hi, Emily, hi Baby Girl!" Riley was holding her hand out to let Baby Girl sniff her, but it was clear she recognized her right away. She was wagging her tail so fiercely that her whole backside was wiggling from side to side.

Emily pulled back on the leash. "Sorry, but this is a good opportunity for her to work on her manners. Let me settle her down before you pet her."

"Of course," Riley smiled.

Baby Girl almost couldn't contain herself, and Emily said, "I swear, this dog doesn't get this excited to see me!"

Finn said, "I'm beginning to think Riley has some canine DNA since she spends so much time with dogs and loves them so much."

This made Riley smile, and Emily laugh. "Do you have dogs of your own?" she asked as she got Baby Girl into a seated position.

Riley felt a lump form in her throat and was grateful that Finn spoke up. "We do, um, but Riley's dog has gone missing."

Emily immediately stopped what she was doing, and Riley saw from her pained expression that she understood how awful this was. "Oh, Riley, I'm so sorry. How long has it been?"

"Six days," Riley choked out. She really didn't want to cry.

Emily's eyes turned sympathetic. "Don't give up. Baby Girl was missing for so long, and we got her back." Emily's expression steeled. "You have to keep reminding people about your dog. Just keep putting info out there. Be a nuisance if you have to, and don't give up hope."

"Thanks," Riley said, feeling more encouraged than she had since Buster went missing. "I've been handing out flyers, there's a stack at the counter, too, and we have a social media page for Buster."

"Buster," Emily said. "Is he a Yorkie?"

Riley nodded. "We rescued him from an illegal puppy mill."

"Oh, wow," Emily said. "I've seen his flyers all over. You're doing a really great job. Don't give up." She smiled down at Baby Girl who was sitting, waiting patiently for attention as her tail swept briskly across the wood floor. "Can you do me a favor? Can you let Baby Girl love on you since she's being so polite?"

Riley smiled. "Of course." She sat down on the floor and shared a private glance with Finn before scratching Baby Girl on her chest. "Hey, Baby Girl," she said in a high voice which the rust-colored dog responded to by licking Riley on the cheek. She wiggled with excitement but stayed in a sit. "You're such a good girl." Baby Girl's tail thumped on the wooden floor when Riley's vision went dark. She could hear Finn detailing to Emily all the things they were doing to find Buster. Good, she thought, glad that Finn knew he might need to distract Emily if Riley felt anything from Baby Girl.

Baby Girl showed her a dark place, and Riley caught an earthy scent. She heard footsteps that sounded like hard soled shoes on dirt, but she didn't feel like she was outside. She felt scared and uncertain while trying to make out her location. For a moment, she felt something familiar and comforting, but then it disappeared. She felt fear - and hatred? She heard a dog's cry, then a whimper. Was it Baby Girl? Something tugged her, and now she skidded along gravel, or was it dirt? Either way, it hurt. She didn't want to go and could feel herself resisting. Her shoulder hit a rough wall. Was that brick?

She heard a click, and light illuminated her surroundings. She saw a tunnel! The tunnel looked just like the one they had been in at the Public House. It had stacked stone walls and a dirt floor. It was narrow and quiet, except for the male voice she heard. "Come on! Get up!"

Riley startled in the present, and Baby Girl scratched at her knee with her paw, as if to make sure she was okay. Riley definitely felt out of sorts and relieved to hear Emily chattering away with Finn. Riley had to compose herself. She felt dizzy and her eyes couldn't focus. She rubbed Baby Girl on either side of her face, her fleshy cheeks, behind her ears, and along her neck, giving her a little doggie massage and calming herself in the process. Finn and Emily stood behind Riley so that Baby Girl faced them. "Oooh, she looks like she's enjoying that," Emily cooed.

Riley smiled but didn't turn around, still trying to clear her head. "Yeah, I think she does." Riley gazed into Baby Girl's dark eyes. She whispered, "You were taken, weren't you?" Baby Girl responded by licking Riley on the end of her nose. Riley reflected on what Baby Girl had just shown her. Someone forcibly moved her somewhere...underground. If this could be related to Buster, and all the other missing dogs, she had to figure out where this happened to Baby Girl. And, if she was in a tunnel, it could be close by.

CHAPTER TWENTY-SIX

Confirmation

Riley felt normal again and stood up after giving Baby Girl one last pet. "I'm so glad we ran into you guys. Seeing Baby Girl gives me renewed hope that we will find Buster, and that he'll be okay."

A concerned look washed over Emily's face, but then quickly disappeared, replaced by a warm smile. "I'm so glad you feel better. Just keep pestering people about him. You are his voice, and maybe someone will see something or know something about where he is."

"Out of curiosity," Riley asked, "where did Baby Girl turn up? I don't think I ever saw it posted on her page."

Emily paused before answering and looked down at her girl. "She was found not far from where she went missing, but I'm afraid I can't say any more since the police are still investigating it."

"Oh, okay," Riley said. "I sure am glad you found her." She tried not to get sad again.

Emily said, "Me too. Just remember, Buster can be found too. Think positively and don't give up on him."

Riley half-smiled. "Thanks."

"Well," Finn said, "we should let you two get going. It

was great seeing you."

"Same here," Emily said as she looked back down at Baby Girl. "I know she enjoyed it very much."

Riley gave Baby Girl one last pet on her head then headed toward the back door that led to the parking lot. Hopefully there were fewer people out there. She needed a moment and some fresh air.

"You okay?" Finn asked. His eyes showed concern as he followed Riley into the parking lot behind the shop.

Riley inhaled a deep breath, then let it out. "Yeah, that was intense." She had her hands on her hips and started pacing. "What do you think the police are investigating regarding Baby Girl?"

Finn looked confused and shook his head. "I don't know."

Riley continued pacing. "Emily said that she couldn't say more about where they found Baby Girl because the police were still investigating."

"Yeah?" Finn replied.

Still pacing, Riley tucked her hair behind her ear and said, "Why would they be investigating her being found? I mean, that would be separate from the incident where she ran off."

A look of realization washed across Finn's face. "You're right."

Riley stopped and looked at Finn. "There's clearly more, and Emily acted a little strange. What else could be going on?"

Finn shrugged his shoulders. "Maybe they think she ended up getting stolen after she ran off? Maybe they are investigating that and the other dogs that have recently gone missing?"

"Maybe," Riley said. "I think I know where we need to start looking."

"Did Baby Girl show you anything that can help?" Finn asked with hopeful eyes.

Riley nodded, "Finn, she was in a tunnel."

"A tunnel?" He asked as his eyes grew wide.

"Yeah, it looked just like the ones we've been in. The floor was dirt, and the walls were stacked stone. She was practically being dragged, and she was scared. So scared." Riley's eyes glazed over as she recalled what the dog had shown her. "I think she was taken, by bad people."

Finn's mouth fell open. "Really?" After Riley nodded, he said, "Then we have to get back into those tunnels!"

"I know, but how?" Riley felt desperate to find a way back in because if someone took Buster, the tunnels may lead them to him. "The Public House is closed. The hatch at Smith Plantation is locked up tight. We have to find out if there's another way into those tunnels."

"I think I can help," said an older, male voice behind them.

Riley jumped and turned to look; it was the old man who lived in the house next to The Downtown Pooch. "Hi! You know about the tunnels?"

The old man hobbled over to them with his cane in his left hand. "I do. I've been in this town my whole life, and we used to play in the tunnels when I was a boy, younger than you!"

Riley couldn't believe her luck. They needed to find out everything this old man knew about the tunnels...and fast.

"Wow," Finn said. "You used to play in the tunnels?"

The old man smiled. "Sure did. We used to have a great time. Of course, Roswell was much different back then. It was a quiet town, not nearly as busy as it is now. This used to be a quiet street, if you can believe that." The old man gestured to Canton Street which was busy with traffic and pedestrians. "Now I've got people walking through my yard, parking in front of my driveway."

Riley wanted to get the man back on topic. "I bet it has changed a lot. How did you get into the tunnels back then?"

"Not far from here is the property that Roswell King owned. It's now a bank on the corner of Magnolia and Mimosa," the old man replied. "He had a log cabin on that property, and it had a root cellar. Well, that root cellar was more than that - it was part of the tunnel system that ran underneath Roswell."

"Wow!" Riley said. "Like the one at Smith Plantation."

The old man looked at her and said, "Yes, there was access to the tunnels from there, too, but it just led to the cook house, not inside Smith Plantation."

"We can't access that one anymore," Finn said. "They've locked it up."

"Well, I'm afraid you won't be able to access the one at the old King property either. When the bank bought that property, they closed up any access to the tunnel system. They couldn't very well have a tunnel that close to their vault."

Riley didn't know her hopes could be dashed so quickly. "So there's no way to access that at all?"

"Nope." The man shifted his weight and placed both hands on his cane. "From what we could tell, and from what we had heard, the tunnels ran in between each of the founding families' homes. Legend has it, that's how they moved messages and even people during the war."

"Wow," Finn said. "That's so cool! We found a tunnel at the Public House. Is it connected?"

The man nodded. "Yep, since that was the company store for the mill, you can imagine they would need to move goods from there as well. In fact, many speculate that is how they moved the fabric for the Confederate soldiers' uniforms, right under the noses of the Yankees. Supposedly, there was a portion of the tunnel that led to the mill, but that was sealed up tight by the time we started exploring." The old man had a wistful look on his face as he recalled the days of being young and spry, finding adventures in the tunnels under their town.

"So," Finn said, "You mentioned that the tunnel at Smith Plantation didn't go into the house. Could you access the other founders' homes from the tunnels?"

The old man nodded his head. "I think so, but I can't say for sure. There are doors throughout the tunnel system, and of course, they are all locked. My friends and I used a compass to determine where we were going and made note of how long it took us to walk as we approached a door. Then, we would walk the route above-ground, and it basically added up. I'm sure those tunnels went in between the founders' homes."

"Did you happen to map this out or keep any notes?" Riley asked hopefully.

"My friend Frank mapped it out and kept all the notes, but sadly he's passed on. I don't know if he would have even hung onto that stuff," the old man said as he rubbed at the short white whiskers on his chin.

Riley had another idea, "So, was the tunnel at Roswell King's property accessed from inside his house, or outside?"

The old man said, "It was inside the home."

Finn's brow wrinkled and he cocked his head. "So, how did you access it?"

"Well, we really shouldn't have. Our parents told us to stay away from the decrepit old log cabin. It really wasn't safe to be in it, but we knew a lot of older kids hung out there at night, so we got curious. It was actually a dare."

Riley tried to imagine this stout old man as an energetic kid. "So, what happened?"

"Frank dared me to go inside, so I did, and right there in the middle of the floor was an open hatch. When I told him about it, he came in with me for a look. We ended up going down into the hatch, and that's when we found the tunnel. There was a door, but it looked like someone, probably the older kids who hung out there, had busted through it to see what was on the other side."

"That's crazy!" Finn said. "It's too bad that hatch entrance isn't accessible anymore."

"The old homestead was overgrown and eventually demolished. Of course, the bank filled in that entrance and sealed everything up."

"Do you know of any entrances to the tunnels that are outside?" Riley asked, then added, "Aside from the one at the cook house at Smith Plantation?"

The old man thought for a moment and said, "Could be, but with the doors off the tunnels being locked, we had no way of knowing for sure. And, our above-ground surveying skills weren't the greatest."

"So," Riley said, "the only way to access the tunnels would be from inside one of the homes?"

"I think so," the old man said. "Of course, we never pursued that route since we could access it through the old homestead."

Riley noticed a change in the man's demeanor, his lips drew tight and his posture stiffened. She thought about her own weird experience in the tunnel. "Why not, did something happen in the tunnels?"

The old man looked at Riley with hard eyes. "Have you read about Roswell King?"

Riley and Finn shook their heads. "No, not much," Riley said.

"I know people think I'm a strange old man, but I got a bad feeling when we were in certain parts of the tunnels." Riley and Finn exchanged glances upon hearing this. They had strange feelings down there too. The man continued, "Roswell King was known to be very hard on his slaves. Some have even described him as a cruel man. All I can think is that some bad things happened in those tunnels."

"Or, maybe his ghost is haunting them," Finn said,

almost without thinking.

"It's quite possible. This town is full of ghosts," the old man said as he looked up at the sky.

Riley couldn't believe it. That might explain why she got sick in the tunnels, but she knew where they had to go to try to get into the tunnel system again - Bulloch Hall. They'd have to figure out a way to explore while her mom was on duty.

CHAPTER TWENTY-SEVEN

Searching for a Tunnel

Riley, Finn, and Eve had to wait until Monday to get into Bulloch Hall while Riley's mom worked. This time, Eve came with them to see if she could help communicate with Mister Oscar, should he appear on the grounds again.

The kids arrived on the porch at nine o'clock sharp and knocked on the door. Riley's mom answered and looked as beautifully put together as always. "Who would have thought you three would be up this early on the first Monday of summer vacation?" Her eyes lit up with her smile when she said this.

"Thanks for letting us come early so we can ghost-hunt," Finn said, his excitement evident by his broad smile and bright eyes. "This is going to be so cool."

"We have an hour until the first tour, so that should give you a decent amount of time to see what you can find. Where do you want to start?"

Riley said, "We don't want to be in your way, and we know you'll be on the first floor, so we thought we might start in the basement. Since we only have an hour, we'll probably just stay down there." Riley hated fibbing to her mom, but they would be ghost hunting. She hoped they actually found an entrance to the tunnel. If it led from inside the house, it had to be somewhere in the basement.

"Sounds good!" her mom said. "Just be careful, okay?"

"We will, Mrs. Carson," Finn said. "We never try to provoke ghosts. We'll just ask questions to try to get them to communicate with us if they are here."

"Mom?" Riley asked. "Can we go into the area that's blocked off with the white picket fence? I guess that was a root cellar."

Her mom smiled, "Of course, you can. Just be careful going down those steps. They're kind of steep, and there aren't any handrails, so we don't let visitors go down there, but you can certainly have a look around. It's really neat to see how they built that into the earth. Imagine not having refrigeration and having to use mother nature to help you store your food."

"That's really cool when you think about it," Eve said. "People had to be really resourceful back then."

"They sure did," Riley's mom said. "They used ropes tied to their bed frames under their mattresses, and mattresses were often filled with straw, dried leaves, corn husks, or horsehair. We demonstrate this on the tour. Hang on, I'll show you." Riley's mom went down the hall and to the master bedroom on the left and returned with three little sachets. "Riley and Finn have already seen these on the tour, but it is what mattresses would have felt like back then."

Eve took each sample and felt them. "Wow, that's crazy. You really can feel a difference between each of these too."

Riley's mom smiled proudly. "You sure can. I'm glad we

have the technology we do, because I don't think I could get a good night's sleep on any of these."

The kids laughed at this and Finn, anxious to get going, said, "Well, we'd better head downstairs so we can be done before your tour starts."

"If you're not, just tuck yourselves away in the educational room when you hear us coming downstairs. Since you two have been on the tour, you know the flow. We won't be in the basement long."

"Thanks, mom," Riley said, and the friends took off to the back of the house and were down the staircase in no time.

"Okay," Finn said, "It only seems logical that a tunnel entrance would be down in that root cellar. There's nothing visible from the kitchen or that educational room, so let's start there."

"Agreed," Riley said as Finn headed to the doorway that was around the side of the staircase and on an interior wall. Finn moved the barrier fence out of the way and let Riley and Eve head down the steps first. When they got downstairs safely, he stepped down the first step and turned around to place the fence exactly where it had been, then joined his friends at the bottom. Dirt covered the floors, and the walls were tall brick with white paint across most of their surface. Riley turned to Finn, "Oh, do you have your recorder going?"

Finn smiled wryly. "Sure do." His mini recorder hung from his neck, and he held it up so Riley could see the red light. He put his hand in his pocket and pulled out the EMF detector. "Do one of you want to monitor this for me?"

"Sure," Eve said and took the device from Finn. "Just let you know if the lights turn red?"

"Yep!" Finn said.

Riley looked around the small space. A cabinet stood against the back wall with pots and vases displayed on its shelves. There were wooden benches along each of the side walls staged with plastic fruits, vegetables, and cooking utensils. Between the bench on the right wall and the cabinet on the back wall sat an old wooden barrel with fake potatoes inside. "Well, this is a pretty small space, and off the bat, I don't see a tunnel entrance."

Finn said, "Let's look behind the cabinet." He walked a few paces to where the old wooden cabinet stood. "If it is behind here, we'd have to be very careful moving it because of all the stuff on it."

"Yeah," Riley agreed. "We can't go moving all kinds of stuff, and we definitely can't break anything."

"I know," Finn said as he clicked his flashlight on. He walked around the barrel to the right side of the cabinet shining his light behind it. "Nope, this looks like a solid brick wall. Luckily the cabinet isn't right up against it, so I can easily see behind it."

The kids surveyed the small room. "Clearly there isn't anything along the two side walls," Riley said. "Unless some of those bricks are fake."

Eve looked along the wall that the stairs were on. "It would make sense if it were on that wall because if there's a tunnel, it would go away from the house, under the kitchen, and then you're in the backyard."

"Good call," Finn said as he eagerly headed to the wall the stairs came off. Riley and Eve joined him to inspect the wall on either side of the staircase.

"Maybe there's something behind the stairs?" Riley suggested, then promptly squatted down to have a look.

Finn crouched on the other side of the staircase inspecting the wall with her. "I don't know. I don't see anything along this area, either."

"I'm gonna crawl through and get a better look," Riley said. As she squeezed through the small space under the stairs, she caught her necklace on something, and the old key fell to the dirt, making an almost hollow sound. "Did you hear that?" she asked her friends.

"Yeah," Finn said, unable to see what made the noise. "What was that?"

"My key! It fell off my neck and landed on the dirt, but I think there's something under here. Give me more light."

Finn and Eve shined their flashlights into the small space under the stairs. Riley picked up the key and re-tied her necklace, then she started sweeping away at the dirt. "Hang on," Eve said, "there's an old broom in here." Eve went to the left wall and grabbed an old broom. It had a short handle like it might have been used in a fireplace to sweep the ashes away. She handed it to Riley who started sweeping the dirt.

After a moment, Finn said, "I see something. Is that a piece of metal?" He pointed to the area closest to the wall, away from the foot of the stairs.

Riley swept some more in that area and said, "Yes! This

might be a hatch." She started to see outlines of a long and narrow rectangle and was able to place her feet on either side to try to pull up on the hatch, but it refused to budge. "Finn, upstairs on the fireplace, there are tools. Can you grab one that we can use to pry this open?"

"Be right back," Finn said as he bounded up the stairs that she crouched under.

Riley crawled out of the small space and brushed her hands off on her jeans when Finn arrived back downstairs with an old iron tool. "That looks perfect. This was so creative," Riley said. "When the hatch is open, I bet it matches the angle of the staircase."

"Oh yeah, you're right," Eve said.

Finn used the iron tool that had a pointed hook on the end to get the leverage he needed to pry open the hatch. It opened with a groaning squeak just like the one at Smith Plantation. "Just like the other one," he said to Riley with a grin. All three kids shined their lights down into the hatch that Finn held open.

"And, just like the other one, a low tunnel with a dirt floor," Riley said, suddenly feeling claustrophobic.

"We should find something to prop the door open with," Finn suggested as he tried to use the iron tool, but it just wasn't long enough.

"Look," Eve said as she shined her light on the back of a stair tread. "Is that so it can hook onto the stair?"

"I bet she's right," Riley said. "There's an iron hook on the back of that stair." She shined her flashlight to join Eve's beam of light so Finn could see better. "Finn, see if the handle for the hatch door will attach to that."

Finn set down the iron tool and used both hands to push the hatch door until it met the back of the stairs. "Yep!" he said as the metal clanked together. "That's so clever."

Now with the hatch held all the way open with the hook, the three friends shined their lights into it. They could make out a short, wooden ladder on one of the long sides of the hatch opening. "Well, that should make it easier to get out of than the other one," Riley said, referring to the one at Smith Plantation that you had to heave yourself out of. "With these stairs in the way, it would be harder to lift yourself out of this one."

"But," Finn said as he went around to the other side, "I bet we can drop down into it from this side." He dug into a pocket on the side of his cargo pants and pulled out a glow stick. Cracking it open, he dropped it into the hatch as they all watched. "It's a short drop. I'll go first." With that, he sat down, dangled his legs into the hole and dropped down. "Oh yeah, it's like four feet or so, an easy drop. Hopefully it opens up like the last one."

Riley looked at Eve, "Are you sure you're cool with this? I got a weird feeling when Finn and I went underground before."

Eve nodded, "I'll be okay. I really want to help."

Riley smiled, knowing that Eve's ability to see ghosts could make this a difficult or uncomfortable experience for her. "Thanks, Eve. I really appreciate it."

Eve sat down just as Finn had and dropped herself into the hole. She stood with her head poking out of the hole, just like Finn had done. "Finn's right, that's an easy drop."

As Eve moved out of the way, Riley said a silent prayer for protection. She unconsciously held her key necklace and said aloud, "Mister Oscar, if you're around today, we'd love to have you join us." Riley knew that the slave ghost had protected her in the past and would feel better if his presence was felt. As she dangled her feet over the side, she heard her mom's voice overhead and footsteps on the stairs to the kitchen. "Just in time," she thought as she hopped into the hole, then got on her hands and knees to join her friends to see where this underground hatch led.

CHAPTER TWENTY-EIGHT

A Way In

Riley, Finn, and Eve crawled about eighteen feet in a low tunnel when it opened up like the one they had been in before. At the point where they could stand, however, they couldn't go any further. An old door with an iron lock blocked their way. "Aw, man," Riley said when she got to where her friends waited for her.

"It won't budge," Finn said giving the door knob a twist and jiggle as he pushed and pulled.

"Do you think we can pick the lock?" Eve suggested. As she said this, the EMF detector in her hand lit up red. "Uh, Finn?" She held up the EMF detector and showed Finn the blinking red lights.

"Oh my gosh," Finn said, "we're getting something!" He looked at Eve's brown eyes, "Are you sensing anything?" Eve's brow furrowed and she cocked her head. "No, I don't feel a thing." She looked back at the EMF detector which was green now, indicating no activity.

"Huh," Finn said as he held out his hand so he could inspect the device. "Maybe it's not a ghost, but a magnetic field or something."

"That's weird," Riley said as she unconsciously clutched

at her key necklace, and then immediately said, "My key!" She slipped the necklace off over her head and said, "Let's try it." Eve stepped to the side so Riley could join Finn by the door. As she stuck the old, iron key into the lock, it felt like it fit. She looked at Finn and said, "It fits!"

Finn clearly didn't want to get his hopes up and said, "It fit in the one at the Public House too, but didn't budge."

Riley turned the key and felt movement. "Who knows when the last time this lock was even used," she said as she used a little more force. Then, with a loud click, the lock turned. Riley pulled out the key and twisted the knob, "It worked!" she said. Her eyes danced with excitement. Riley pushed the door forward, and it felt like it had been closed for a very long time. She pushed harder and the door opened into a larger tunnel.

Finn's mouth hung agape as he took in the sight. "Who knew that key that you've been wearing all this time would actually work a lock that we needed to unlock?" His eyes sparkled with excitement now too.

"This is so cool!" Eve said as she joined her friends in the large tunnel.

"Let's close it up as we investigate, and I'll leave another glow stick right by it. It can get disorienting down here so I want to make sure we mark where we need to go to get out." Finn closed the door and set a glow stick where the door met the tunnel wall.

"Which way should we go?" Riley asked her friends. At this point, they could go left or right. Since they had no map of the tunnel system, they had no idea which way would be the best way to go.

Eve said, "Something is pulling me to go right."

"Do you sense anything?" Finn asked?

Eve shook her head. "No, it's more like intuition."

"Then, right it is," Finn said as the three friends shined their flashlights out in front of them. Finn pulled a compass out of a cargo pant pocket and held it in the palm of his hand while they walked. "Okay," he said, "we're going northeast."

Riley thought for a moment. "So, in the direction of our neighborhood."

"Yep," Finn said. "I wonder if we'll cross under Magnolia?"

Eve said, "Well, if the old man was right, we should cross under it at some point if this tunnel leads to Roswell King's old property."

"That's right," Riley said. "That bank is on the other side of Magnolia."

"That'll be a decent walk if we want to go that far. Do you guys want to check out that section to see how they closed it up when the bank was built?" Finn asked.

"We might as well," Riley said. "Let's just follow this as far as we can go and look for clues about dogs. I know Baby Girl showed me a tunnel for a reason."

"We may as well do a little ghost hunting while we're at it, don't you think?" Finn suggested eagerly.

Riley smiled. "Of course, we can multi-task." Secretly, she hoped that ghost hunting might take her mind off her unease about being in the tunnels and why Baby Girl wanted to show this to her.

Finn looked at Eve. "Are you okay with this too?"

Eve nodded. "Of course."

After Finn told Eve how they do an EVP session, he began. "Hello? Is there anyone in this tunnel who would like to communicate with us?" The kids stayed silent a few moments in case there was a response.

"We're friendly," Riley said. "Have you seen any dogs down here?"

Finn checked the EMF detector which monitors magnetic fields and could indicate the presence of a ghost. "Right now, this isn't picking up on anything. How about you, Eve?"

Eve shook her head. "Nope, so far, nothing."

As they continued walking, Finn stopped abruptly. "My pedometer! I forgot to set it!" They had discussed how they could track the number of steps they walked underground and try to figure out their location when they were above ground, similar to what the old man and his friends did so many years ago.

"It's okay," Riley said. "I started mine when I got into the hatch."

"Cool," Finn said. "I'm checking my compass periodically to see if we have any direction changes."

"It's too bad we don't get cell service down here," Eve said. "Then we could just use GPS."

"I know. That would make life easier," Riley said as the trio continued walking down the dark, musty tunnel.

"How many steps have we taken?" Finn asked.

Riley pulled out her phone to check, "Two hundred and

twenty. We haven't gone too far."

"Eve, are you getting anything at all?" Finn asked.

Eve said, "It feels a little heavy down here, but I'm not sensing any spirits at this point."

Riley fidgeted with her key which hung around her neck. "Maybe that's a good sign."

"Look!" Finn said. His flashlight scanned the rough, stone wall on their right. "Is that another door?"

On their right stood another wooden door with an old iron lock. "This is so cool," Riley said.

"Should we check it out?" Finn asked.

Riley thought for a moment. "Let's check it out on the way back. Since we have to come back this way anyway, we can see where it goes then. I feel like we should get an idea of where the main tunnel goes first."

"I agree," Eve said. "I'll make notes so we can map this out later. Let's continue on the main tunnel."

"This is rad!" Finn said. "We didn't find nearly this much in the tunnel that led south from Smith Plantation."

"Well, this seems to be the side of the street with all the big, fancy homes, so it makes sense," Eve said referring to the fact that back then, Smith Plantation was the only large home near here that occupied the other side of the square; the side Eve and her family lived on now.

"It's definitely where the founders were more concentrated," Riley said as she thought about the smaller homes that the mill workers lived in on the other side of the square.

Finn looked at his compass. "We're still heading northeast."

Eve said, "Got it," as she made a note in her phone.

Riley shuddered involuntarily. "Eve, do you feel anything?"

"Stop," Eve said as she stood in place, and Riley and Finn stopped and looked at her.

"What is it?" Finn asked. He pulled out his EMF detector, which was now flashing red lights.

"I heard someone say stop," Eve said. She looked around in the dark tunnel. "It's hard to see anything, but I feel a presence." She turned her head as if to see if she could hear or sense anything else. Suddenly, her head came to a stop. "It's Mister Oscar. He said, 'It's okay, chil'.'"

Riley felt her heart flutter. "Where is he?" she asked, excited that their guardian angel was with them. "Hi, Mister Oscar," she said.

"I can't see him," Eve said. "He may not have the energy to manifest himself, but he's here. And, he responded, he said, 'Hello, chil', after you spoke to him."

Riley felt butterflies in her belly and her mouth turned upward. She thought back to the day Mister Oscar had somehow manifested enough energy to appear at Vickery Creek and pull her from the rushing water, saving her life. She loved this man who seemed keen to protect them.

"Mister Oscar," Finn said eagerly. "Thank you for being here and watching over us. Is there anything you need to communicate with us?"

They remained silent waiting for a response. Riley hoped that Eve would be able to hear.

"He said, 'Wait here. Stay still,'" Eve replied in a whisper.

Riley and her friends stood as still as statues, quietly waiting, but for what, they were not sure. Riley felt her nerves in her stomach. She knew she could trust Mister Oscar, but the fact that he appeared meant something. She wasn't sure if it was something good or bad.

After what seemed like an eternity, but was probably only five minutes, they heard something. A distant whine. When Riley heard it, she stilled even more, closed her eyes, and tilted her head to listen more closely. Then, another louder whine, and this time, it sounded like a dog. Riley gasped involuntarily and quickly put her hand over her mouth.

Eve looked at Riley and gave her the 'Shh' sign, placing her index finger in front of her lips. Her dark amber eyes turned serious. Next, they heard scraping as if something was being dragged across the dirt floor. The three friends remained silent. After about five more minutes, Eve said, "We can go. Mister Oscar said, 'Go now chil'. Find him.'"

Riley's heart began to beat in her chest. "Find who?"

"I don't know," Eve said softly. "That's all he said."

"Let's keep going and see what we find," Finn said. "Let's just move carefully and quietly, okay?"

Riley and Eve nodded in agreement, and Eve asked Riley, "Are you okay with going?"

Eve knew Riley worried about what they might find after what Mister Oscar just said. She felt her eyes well with tears and tucked her hair behind her ear nervously. "Yes, we need to see what's down there."

The three friends scanned the tunnel with their flashlights as they silently walked toward the noises they heard, uncertain of what they would find. The only noise they could hear was the sound of their footsteps on the dirt floor. Thoughts swirled in Riley's head. Thoughts she would normally share with her friends but felt too scared to verbalize. Clearly, they all felt they should be as quiet as possible while they continued down the tunnel. Why had Mister Oscar told them to be quiet? What was down here? Was it something supernatural as she had felt before in the other section of the tunnel? Whatever that was, it had made her feel sick to her stomach, and it even affected Finn. She wasn't feeling any of that now, thank goodness, but she felt extremely anxious. What if Mister Oscar referred to Buster when he said, "Find him?"

Riley and her friends walked for about 400 feet since they heard those noises, and Finn noticed something. "Look," he said quietly, but excitedly. "There are paw prints in the dirt."

Riley felt her heart speed up as she knelt next to Finn to inspect the prints which were close to the rough stone wall. She felt conflicted when she saw the paw prints. "They're larger than Buster's," she said, half relieved and half disappointed.

"Maybe they're Baby Girl's?" Finn suggested.

Eve joined them to inspect the prints as well and noted this so they could analyze it later. "We should pay attention to where we walk and keep our eyes peeled for anything else that could be a clue."

Riley stood and used her light to scan the immediate area. "This is weird."

"What?" Finn asked as he stood to survey the ground

with her.

"What do you notice about the paw prints?" She asked and Eve stood to join them.

Finn scanned the area. "They're random. If a dog was walking down here, they would be in a line, but they're not."

"Exactly," Riley said. "They're sporadic. There is no pattern."

Finn walked to the center of the tunnel and shined his flashlight around the dirt floor, then kicked at the ground. "The dirt is thin in most places, except near the walls." He walked from the center of the tunnel to the opposite wall and kicked at the dirt. "It's much thicker along the walls, so that's where we're likely going to see prints."

"Then they just disappear," Eve said. She moved ahead of her friends and carefully scanned the ground.

Riley and Finn joined Eve. "That's so weird," Riley said as they continued to scan the ground.

Finn appeared intrigued because he continued searching the ground in front of them. "There's nothing here," he said.

Riley went back to the paw prints they had found and searched the area more closely, this time, examining the left wall closest to the prints. After a few moments, she said, "There's something here on the wall."

Finn arrived at the wall in a flash, facing Riley. They both crouched low, and Eve joined them, squatting across from them. Her light shined straight out at the wall in front of her. "Where?" she asked.

Riley pointed to a dark spot on the rough, stacked stone wall about twelve inches above the ground. "Right here.

What is that?"

Finn swiped his finger across the dark smear on the wall and pulled his finger away. Shining in the lights of their three flashlights was Finn's finger stained red. "Looks like blood," he said.

Riley inhaled sharply. "Oh my gosh. Is there an injured dog down here?"

"If there is," Eve said, "then someone must have picked it up, because there's no trace of it walking around down here."

"We have to find it," Riley said quietly, but eagerly.

"Let's keep going down the tunnel," Finn suggested. "If someone was carrying it, they didn't come past us."

Riley and Eve agreed as they stood to continue down the tunnel. The friends started walking and had gone about fifteen feet down the tunnel when Eve stopped abruptly. "Wait, stop."

"What is it?" Riley asked with concern.

"Mister Oscar. He says to go back," Eve said.

"Go back?" Finn asked. "But that doesn't make sense."

"He's serious," Eve said, as her brow wrinkled and she eyed her friends nervously. "He's really worried, guys."

This made Riley's stomach flip. "If Mister Oscar is worried, we should listen to him."

"But we know a dog, or someone carrying a dog, didn't go past us," Finn said as frustration crept into his voice. "The dog has to be this way." He shined his light down the direction they headed.

"I know," Riley said, "But Mister Oscar has only ever

helped us. We need to trust him."

"You're sure it's Mister Oscar?" Finn asked, looking at Eve earnestly.

"Yes," Eve nodded, her eyes wide. "We need to go. He just said, 'Go back. Get home.'"

Riley looked at Finn, "I'm going. We're either not safe down here or something else is going on, but Mister Oscar has saved me more than once."

Finn hesitated, then agreed. "You're right. This may not make sense, but you're right. We have to trust him." And with that, the three friends quickly headed back to the hatch under Bulloch Hall.

CHAPTER TWENTY-NINE

Following Mister Oscar

The kids got back to the door which led to the hatch in the cellar of Bulloch Hall without seeing or hearing anything else. They didn't have time to investigate the other door on their way back, and after they closed and locked the door leading to the main tunnel, they quietly made their way through the low tunnel and back into the root cellar at Bulloch Hall. Riley looked at the clock on her phone. "My mom should just be finishing up the tour, so our timing is perfect."

Finn climbed out of the hatch last, and as he unhooked the hatch door from the underside of the stairs, he said, "Let's head to my house so we can listen to what we recorded down there. Maybe we caught something that we didn't hear."

"That's a good idea," Eve said. She looked around the root cellar. "Does everything look as it did when we came down here?"

Riley nodded after surveying the space. "Yeah, I'll set the broom back and Finn, can you put that fireplace tool back when we go up?"

"Yep," Finn said as he raised the tool in his hand. He already thought of it and was eager to get going.

As the kids neared the top of the stairs leading to the first floor, Riley could hear her mom bidding farewell to her tour group. She stopped at the top of the stairs, indicating for her friends to stay behind her. After they heard the wooden front door close, Riley peeked out into the hallway. "Is the coast clear?" she asked her mom.

"Hey honey," her mom said as the kids joined her in the foyer. "I was wondering if y'all would be down there much longer. How did it go? Did you capture anything?"

"I'm sure we did," Finn said. "I can't wait to get home and listen to see what we got."

"Well, I hope it's nothing scary," Riley's mom said. "If there are ghosts around here, hopefully they mean well."

"I'm sure they do," Eve said with a knowing look and sweet smile. "A lot of times, spirits are just so imprinted on a place they really loved, and I bet that's the case here."

"Thanks for letting us come investigate," Riley said to her mom.

"Anytime, Roo," her mom said with a quick squeeze around Riley's shoulders. "My next tour starts in five minutes, so I'm going to grab some water. All this talking really makes you thirsty."

"We'll let you get that water," Finn said. "And sit for a few minutes before your next tour."

"You sure are eager to listen to those recordings, aren't you?" Riley's mom said with good spirit.

Finn smiled sheepishly. "Yeah, I do get pretty excited about this stuff."

Riley's mom smiled. "I know." She opened the front door for them. "You three go listen to what you caught, and

Riley can tell me all about it tonight."

"Thanks, mom!" Riley said as she and her friends headed out the door and down the front porch steps.

As they walked down the gravel driveway, Finn said, "It's so cool to think we were somewhere under where we're walking now."

"I know," Riley said. "I want to figure out where these tunnels go." She looked at her friends eagerly. "Like what's behind the door we passed, but didn't have time to check out on the way back." She thought about Mister Oscar's eagerness for them to leave the tunnel and looked at Eve. "Eve, do you have any idea why Mister Oscar wanted us to get out of the tunnel?"

Eve shook her head. "None. But not only did he tell us to get out, he said to get home. Don't you think that's kind of weird?"

"That's right," Finn said as they walked through the open gate at the end of the driveway and onto the asphalt of Bulloch Avenue. "I wonder why he said that. The whole thing didn't make much sense."

"Hey, wait," Riley said as she stopped in front of Mimosa Hall. Finn and Eve stopped and looked at her. "If that old man is right and the tunnels connected the founders' homes, maybe that door we didn't get to investigate leads here." She pointed at the grand old home with the impressive landscaping. "Mimosa Hall was the Dunwody family's home, so it would make sense."

"That totally makes sense," Finn said.

"Uh...hey guys?" Eve said with apprehension in her

voice.

Riley and Finn looked at Eve expectantly. "What's up?" Finn asked.

Eve looked down the street, and Riley followed her eyes, seeing nothing but cars parked along one side. Eve said, "It's Mister Oscar. I see him now. He's waving us down the street. We need to go."

Neither Riley nor Finn saw anything, but they trusted what Eve saw, and they quickly followed her down the street. Finn turned his voice recorder on just in case. When they arrived at the end of the street, facing the square and its beautiful park, Riley said, "Which way?"

Eve's head snapped to the left, and she headed in that direction. "This way. Mister Oscar just said, 'This way, chil.'"

The three friends headed quickly down Mimosa Street, in the direction of Riley and Finn's neighborhood. "Do you still see him?" Finn asked.

"Every now and then," Eve said. "It's like he wants to make sure we're following but doesn't have the energy to completely manifest."

Riley hurried ahead. "I bet he used so much of his energy helping us in the tunnel."

The kids got to the end of the square and the intersection of Park Square Court on their right. "Do you still see him?" Finn asked Eve.

"No, I wonder if we should keep going or turn right to head to my neighborhood?" Eve wondered aloud.

Riley looked to her left where an old home sat shielded by thick foliage in its front yard. She fidgeted with her key necklace when Eve said, "This way!" and continued briskly down the sidewalk they were standing on. Eve looked far down the street. "He's up there."

The kids jogged past the driveway of the old home and past the pretty white home with a large front porch that housed a business of some sort. When they got to the white fencing in front of Primrose Cottage, an event facility, Riley asked, "Do you still see him?"

"No," Eve called through quick breaths as they all jogged, "but he was all the way down at the church when I last saw him."

"Is he just leading us home to our neighborhood?" Finn asked referring to where he and Riley lived.

They got to the front of Roswell First Baptist Church. Eve stopped and looked around to see if they were still going the right way. "This is where he was. Right in front of the church."

As Eve faced down the street to see if they should continue straight, Finn looked around the front of the church. Riley turned and looked across the street. The trees that lined the street on the far side casted speckled shadows onto the asphalt, and she thought she saw something. She crossed the street using the crosswalk and focused on something in the road, in front of a storm drain. "Oh my gosh, you guys. Come quick." Riley jogged down the sidewalk and cried out, "Come quick, please!" Lying in the street in front of her was a black dog, and he was in bad shape.

CHAPTER THIRTY

A Residual Haunting

As Finn and Eve joined Riley, they saw what distressed her so. At her feet lay a black dog, which looked like a pit mix. "What should we do?" Riley said, crying at the sight of the poor dog and too scared to touch it.

"I'm calling my dad," Eve said. "We need to be careful. It could bite us."

"I don't even know if it's alive," Riley cried.

Finn squatted next to her and ever so gently, laid his fingertips on the dog's side. "I think it's breathing. Barely, but I think it's still alive."

"Dad!" Eve said into her phone, on the verge of tears herself. "We're on Mimosa near..." she looked at the nearest intersection which they had crossed when they ran over, "near Oxbow Road, and there's a dog in the road. It's in pretty bad shape. Can you come here quickly?" Eve looked at her friends and said, "My dad says not to touch it. Don't try to move it." She went back to listening to her phone. "Okay, thanks dad. We will."

"What did he say?" Riley asked through sobs.

"He'll be here in a minute. He's really close by," Eve said. "Come here." Riley stood and walked into the comforting arms of her friend. "It's okay. My dad will help."

Finn stood guard in front of the dog in case any cars headed down the quiet street. "Do you think it got hit by a car?" He asked his friends who stood on the sidewalk.

"Probably," Eve said as she rubbed a hand up and down Riley's back.

Riley heard a car drive up Oxbow Road. "There's your dad. He's here!" She waved her hands at the unmarked police car, and it turned right onto the street. Finn indicated where the dog lay just behind him.

Eve's dad got out of the driver's side, and his partner, Glen, got out of the passenger's side. "Thanks for getting here so quickly, dad," Eve said.

Detective Rycroft and Glen walked over to where Finn was standing while Riley stood frozen on the sidewalk. "He's just as we found him," Finn said. "He's still breathing, but barely."

"Did you touch the dog?" Detective Rycroft asked.

"Yeah, just softly, to see if it was still alive," Finn said.

"You've gotta be real careful doing that," Glen said, "An injured dog can bite out of fear."

Finn said quietly as he looked down at the dog who had marks and cuts all over his face, "He's really hurt. He didn't even flinch when I touched him."

Detective Rycroft patted Finn on the shoulder, "Thanks, Finn." Then he spoke so only Finn could hear. "Why don't you guys get Riley out of here. She seems pretty upset about seeing this." With that, he squatted down to look at the dog while Glen took pictures.

Finn headed over to Riley and Eve. "They're going to take it from here. There's nothing more we can do. Let's head to my house."

"Do you think he'll be okay?" Riley called out to the men.

Detective Rycroft looked at Riley; his expression seemed grave. "We're going to get him to a vet ASAP. We'll do the best we can."

Riley sniffed. "Thank you." The three friends crossed the street and headed toward Finn's house.

Riley, Finn, and Eve were joined by Molly in Finn's basement, and she stuck by Riley's side. "That poor dog," Riley said as she wiped a tear from her cheek with one hand and stroked Molly's back with the other. "It looked awful."

Eve nodded solemnly. "It was in pretty rough shape. I hope the vet can help."

Finn looked at Riley, and she noticed a look of grave concern quickly cross his face. "I hate that it had to be us who found the dog, but maybe it's a good thing. Eve's dad got there super-fast, and maybe the vet can help." He turned to his laptop and said, "I think we all need a distraction. Let's delve into these recordings and see what we got."

Eve said, "You two listen to the recordings, and I'm going to look at my notes and map out where we think the tunnel was running."

"Good idea," Riley said, grateful for the distraction. "I'll text you the number of steps we took. I'm glad I remembered to check it when we got back into the cellar."

As Eve worked on mapping the tunnel, Riley and Finn shared headphones and listened to Finn's recording. Molly laid at their feet.

The kids worked quietly. Riley and Finn heard everything that Eve had reported to them from Mister Oscar. His voice comforted Riley. When Mister Oscar got agitated and anxious for them to leave the tunnel, Riley felt anxious in the present. She said to Finn, "He really was upset and wanted us out of there. He really looks after us."

Finn nodded as they continued to listen. "I wish we knew what we heard. Remember when we heard what we thought was a dog in the tunnels before, but then we just felt an evil presence?"

Riley nodded as she unconsciously petted Molly and thought back to the noises they heard in the tunnel on the other side of the town square. "It could have been a dog, another animal, or a spirit. We never found out because the tunnel entrance got locked."

Eve looked up with concern in her eyes. "I didn't feel anything other than Mister Oscar's presence, but he could have been warning us if something was heading our way."

Riley thought for a moment, "He was definitely anxious for us to leave. We just have to figure out why."

Riley and Finn turned back to the recording and listened as they argued about leaving. Finn really hadn't wanted to abandon their search so soon. They heard Eve's voice say, "We need to go. He just said, 'Go back. Get home.'" Then, Riley's voice said, "I'm going. We're either not safe down here or something else is going on, but Mister Oscar has saved me more than once."

There was a brief silence before Finn agreed to leave, and in that quiet moment, Riley heard something. "Wait," she said, "go back."

Finn reversed the recording, and they listened closely. "I hear it," Finn said. "It's faint, but I hear a voice, and it doesn't sound like Mister Oscar."

Eve looked up from the paper she used to map the tunnel. "Can you hear what it says?"

"Barely," Finn said. "I'm going to listen through my good headphones and enhance it." He unplugged the ear buds he and Riley shared and plugged in his good headphones.

Eve said to Riley, "Do you think someone was down there with us?"

Riley looked skeptical. "I don't know. It was very quiet, almost a whisper."

Finn clicked at his laptop, and after a few minutes, he sat bolt upright. His eyes shined with glee. He handed Riley the headphones. "Here, have a listen."

Riley put the headphones on and closed her eyes, listening intently. At once, her eyes sprung open. "Oh my gosh!"

Eve scooted to the edge of her seat, anxious to have a listen. Her eyes looked bright with anticipation. "I wanna hear." Riley handed her the headphones as she and Finn wrote down what they had heard. They watched Eve as her dark eyes went wide and her mouth hung open. "I totally didn't hear that when we were down there."

Finn handed her a blank pad of paper. "Write down

what you heard." Eve grabbed her pen and scribbled quickly, and then they all showed each other what they had written. All three had written the same thing. "We have to hide Jefferson's money."

"This is crazy," Riley said.

Eve looked at Finn. "Do you think someone was down there with us?"

Finn shook his head. "Nope, I think this is a residual haunting."

"What's that?" Eve asked.

Riley answered, "It's like a song on repeat. Something happened that was emotional or traumatic, and the energy was left behind. Repeating it over and over."

"Do we know anyone from around here named Jefferson?"

Riley shook her head. "Not that I can think of."

Finn looked up, his eyes thoughtful. After a moment, he looked at his friends. "Jefferson Davis was the president of the Confederate states. What if the tunnel was used to move his money? That would have been a big deal for the Confederates and knowing that Roswell was under siege, whoever was hiding it would have been under a lot of stress to make sure that money stayed safe."

"No way," Riley said. "You think that's what this is about?"

"It makes sense," Finn said. "Remember we watched that show where they were looking for lost Confederate treasure?"

Riley nodded, and it dawned on her. "Yes! Jefferson

Davis supposedly left Virginia when the war was ending. He had gold, silver, and Confederate money and was caught somewhere in South Georgia."

"Is that true?" Eve asked.

Finn shrugged his shoulders and said, "He did flee Virginia and was caught in South Georgia, but when they caught him, he only had a few coins on him, not the wagons full of treasure they suspected he had. No one really knows for sure, but people have been hunting for that lost treasure ever since."

"So, if this residual haunting is talking about 'Jefferson's money'..." Riley used air quotes when she said those last two words.

Finn finished her statement, "Then, maybe Roswell is where some of his money went! Think about it. He was caught without the money, so they had to have unloaded it somewhere along the way. Maybe some of that money came to Roswell?"

Eve was clearly as excited as Riley and Finn now. "You guys, we have to go back and look!"

"This could be what Mr. Powell's clue is about!" Riley said as excitement danced in her eyes.

"Let's see if we can go back tomorrow!" Finn said.

CHAPTER THIRTY-ONE

A Huge Find

Riley and Finn met Eve on Mimosa Street near the town square and today, Tim Harrington joined her. "Hey guys!" Riley said as they approached Eve and Tim.

Finn said to Tim, "So, your grounding is finally over?" He referred to the trouble Tim got into when he spray-painted city hall with Riley's design that meant to bring attention to the breed-specific legislation when it was first passed in Roswell.

Tim hung his head. "Yeah, my dad is finally loosening up on me. What I did was wrong and stupid. Having to clean spray paint off city hall was *not* easy."

The kids chuckled at this and headed down Mimosa toward Bulloch Avenue. "I'm so glad your mom is working again today," Eve said to Riley. "I'm anxious to see if we can find anything related to Jefferson Davis' treasure."

"Me too," Riley said as they made the right turn onto Bulloch Avenue. "I want to see if there are any signs of dogs being in the tunnels."

Tim was clearly interested in treasure too and said, "So, you guys really think what you heard could be related to Jefferson Davis?"

Finn said, "Yeah, I mean, if we find out there was some-one else with the name Jefferson around here, then maybe not, but those tunnels would have definitely been used to move things secretly, especially during the Civil War."

"That would be so cool," Tim said, his eyes bright with excitement.

When they arrived at Bulloch Hall, Riley's mom waited for them on the front porch, sitting in a black rocking chair. She waved at them when she saw them at the end of the long driveway. Upon seeing her, the kids jogged up the gravel drive and were all smiles as they bounded up the front steps.

"Thanks for letting us do more ghost hunting," Finn said as they stepped onto the porch.

"Of course," Riley's mom said as she opened the wooden front door. "I think it's neat you caught something yesterday. Are you going to stay in the cellar again?"

Riley did not want to lie to her mom, and she knew her friends didn't want to either. When she was about to answer, Tim chimed in. "Yeah, we'll stick to the cellar and the area around it. We'll be out of sight so we won't disrupt your tours."

Riley was grateful as her mom smiled and walked them toward the back of the house. "Just be careful, and if you come across a bad spirit, stop and let me know."

Riley smiled at her mom, "We sure will, mom. Hopefully we won't encounter anything bad."

"Yeah," Finn said, "what we captured last time seems to be a residual haunting. An impression left that repeats over and over, so nothing harmful."

Riley's mom checked her watch. "Good." She smiled at them. "Have fun."

Riley led the way as she and her friends descended the back staircase that led to the basement kitchen. They turned right into the kitchen and back to the wall with the opening to the root cellar. Finn moved the picket fence that kept tourists out of this area, and Riley, Eve, and Tim headed down the steep wooden steps that hid the hatch to the tunnel. Finn followed right behind them with the iron tool from the fireplace in the kitchen.

"Okay," Finn said, "I'm starting my recorder, and Riley, you start your pedometer when you get into the hatch." He looked at Tim and handed him his EMF detector. "You monitor this. When it turns from green to red, it could mean that a spirit is around us or that we're close to a magnetic field. Eve, you continue to make notes so you can map where we think these go. I'll have my compass out so I can let you know when we change direction."

"Perfect," Eve said. "I'll also let you know if I hear anything."

Tim looked at her. "Are you sure you're cool with this?"

Eve smiled. "Yeah, we didn't experience anything bad last time, just Mister Oscar who helped us. Besides, I really want to see if we can find anything that might be related to Jefferson Davis' treasure."

Finn smiled. "Awesome." With that, Riley grabbed the broom and cleared away the dirt they had swept back over the hatch door, and Finn used the tool from the fireplace to pry open the hatch door and latched it to the hardware on the back of the stairs. He looked at Riley and motioned to the hatch opening. "You first, so you can unlock the door."

Riley hopped into the hatch and crawled along the dirt floor until the ceiling rose and the door appeared. She was glad she and Finn brought small headlamp flashlights this time. It would make things easier so they could free up their hands. Riley slipped her necklace off her neck and unlocked the door. Mister Oscar had to have left this key for us, she thought to herself as she slipped it back over her head, clutching it tightly for a moment. Soon enough, her friends were with her, with Finn bringing up the rear. As they had done before, they turned right and headed in the direction they had gone last time.

As they made their way down the tunnel, Riley scanned the ground for paw prints or any sign of a dog. "So far, I'm not seeing any paw prints or anything," she said. "I feel like I don't even see distinct footprints either, even though we were down here yesterday."

Tim toed at the ground with his sneaker. "It's pretty hard, and there's not a lot of dirt. I'm surprised you even saw paw prints on this."

Finn said, "The prints were closer to the wall where dirt had settled, but you're right." He scanned the ground with his flashlight. "You can't even see our own tracks from yesterday."

"Well, I'll keep looking," Riley said, "Especially when we

get close to where we were yesterday."

Eve said, "We should be pretty close. I set my pedometer too, and I think we're nearly there."

"If we didn't track our steps, it would be really hard to know where we were down here," Riley said, "I wonder if we'll even be able to spot the place where we found the paw prints - and the blood."

They continued a little further and Finn said, "I think I see it." He stopped and crouched down, shining his light on the rough stone wall. "Here's a dark spot and," he shined his light around the dirt, "yep, here are the paw prints."

Tim squatted down next to him and touched at the dirt right up against the wall beyond the paw prints. "You're right, the dirt is thicker against the wall." He looked at Riley. "That's probably the only place we'll see paw prints or tracks of any kind."

After Finn and Tim stood, they all continued down the tunnel. Riley said a silent prayer that if a dog was down here and hurt, that it got help. Finn continued to monitor his compass as they walked, and Riley scanned the dirt with her hand-held flashlight in the area closest to the tunnel wall. "Okay, we have a change in direction," Finn said. "We're heading more north than east now."

"Cool," Eve said as she made a note in her notebook. "We've gone just over three-thousand steps."

"I see something," Riley said as she quickly squatted down and had her flashlight right where the floor met the wall. "It looks round and metallic." She wiped away some dirt, "It's definitely round. I wonder if it's a dog tag." She continued to scrape away at the dirt as Finn shined his light on the object.

"It looks like it's wedged into the ground on its side," Finn said.

"Yeah, it does. It's definitely round," she said as she pinched it between her thumb and forefinger. "It has writing or something, and there are indentations." She worked the object back and forth, finally freeing it from the ground.

"Wow, that's big," Finn said as he looked at the object which was crusted in hard dirt. "Is it a coin, like a silver dollar?"

"No, I don't think so," Riley said. "It feels like it has two pieces." She pressed on the metal object that was roughly the diameter of the top of a soda can. "One side is flat and the other has a knob or something on the back." Riley used her thumbs to gently scrape off dirt. "There are lines and letters." She inspected the object closely. "And some kind of abbreviation in a fancy font."

"Can you make out what the letters spell?" Eve asked.

Riley said, "I don't think they spell anything. I think it's the alphabet." She flipped the disk over and wiped the dirt off the other side.

Finn crouched right next to Riley, inspecting the metal disk. "Is that a dial?" He pointed to the center of the disk. "Here," he said as he grabbed a bottle of water out of the side of his backpack. "Let's pour a little water over it."

Riley held the metal disk in the palm of her hand as Eve and Tim crouched down so that they were almost in a circle. Finn poured a little water over the disk and something else appeared. "Richmond, Virginia!" Tim said, reading the line of text on the bottom. "That's cool. I wonder if that's where it was made?"

"What does it say above it?" Eve asked.

Riley inspected the disk closely. "It looks like 'F-L-A...'" She used her fingertip to gently work away more dirt. "B-A-R-R-F?"

Tim chuckled, "Florida barrf? Sounds like they weren't Gator fans either."

Finn laughed and said, "No, I think there's a dot after the first 'F.'"

"I think you're right," Riley said as she smoothed her thumb over the 'F' at the end. "Oh, wait, this is actually an 'E,' I think."

Finn looked closely. "Yeah, that looks like an 'E' at the end, not an 'F.' It's in all-caps."

Eve tapped at her phone to make a note. "So, that should be F. LABARRE, RICHMOND, VA. It's gotta be the maker and the place it was made."

"This is so cool," Riley said as she flipped the disk back over. "Okay, so let's check out this side."

"It looks like the alphabet goes around it twice, once in the large circle, and once in the smaller circle," Tim said.

Finn looked closely and spoke quickly, "I think I know what this is! I think that dial on the back helps you turn these two disks," he said, pointing at the circles with the alphabet embossed on them.

"What does it say in the middle?" Eve asked pointing to where there seemed to be a calligraphic font.

Riley thumbed away more dirt, and Finn poured a little water over it and read aloud, "C-S-A, and underneath," he inspected the disk really closely, "S-S! You guys, if this is what I think it is, it's a huge find!" Finn could hardly contain himself.

"What does it mean?" Eve asked.

Riley said, "Confederate States of America, right?"

"Yep," Finn nodded, bobbing his head quickly, and an eager smile spanned the width of his face. "And the S-S stands for Secret Service!"

"No way!" Tim said.

Finn nodded and plucked the disk from Riley's hands. He held the disk in the fingertips of his left hand and used his right fingers to turn the dial on the back. They could hear dirt scratching as he turned it. "This was used to decode messages. It's proof that a Confederate soldier or spy was in these tunnels!"

"This is so cool." Riley said again. "I can't believe we found something like this!"

It was clear that Tim had gotten treasure hunter's fever when he said, "We've gotta look for more stuff. Maybe Jefferson Davis' treasure did come through here."

CHAPTER THIRTY-TWO

A Productive Search

Finn made a note of his compass bearings, and Eve put this information into the notes in her notebook along with the number of steps they had taken. "We definitely want to record this spot," Finn said, then he seemed to have a thought. "Let's make some kind of mark here that we can look for later." He dug into his backpack and pulled out what looked like a marker. "This is a chalk pen. I'll make a little mark here at eye-level and then one down here." He squatted to where Riley had uncovered the disk and made another mark. "In the off-chance that someone actually comes down here, they won't be able to see these marks, and we can use it to verify our location when we come back down here."

"Yep," Eve said, "I've got the steps and your compass reading noted, so that should get us to the area, and if we're a little off, we can look for those marks."

Tim shined his light on the wall and agreed. "You're right. If you're not looking for them, you can't see them, and I don't think anyone would be inspecting the walls down here."

With that, the kids set off down the tunnel. All four of them now scanned the ground earnestly, hoping to find some sort of treasure.

After a while, they started to get tired and came up empty. "I feel like all I see is dirt," Riley said. "It's like I've been looking at the ground for too long."

"I know," Eve agreed, "but I don't want to not look and miss something."

Tim's gaze remained fixated; he hadn't chatted with them and stayed laser focused on searching. Something caught his eye, and he jogged forward and leaned down on the left side of the tunnel, right by the wall. "Is there something on the wall?" Riley asked, afraid they might find more blood. She instinctively started looking for paw prints just in case.

"I swear I saw a sliver of gold on the wall," Tim said, unable to contain his excitement.

"Really?" Finn asked as he joined Tim and shined his light in the area Tim searched.

"I thought I did," Tim said, sounding more doubtful now, "but my eyes are kind of tired of looking."

"Why don't we shut our flashlights off for a minute and rest our eyes? Then we can turn them back on, and all focus on this spot." Eve suggested.

"Good idea," Riley agreed.

The four friends all turned off their lights and stood in the dark. "I'm sure I saw something," Tim said. "This is so cool."

After a few moments, Eve said, "Okay, let's turn our lights back on and scan the area where Tim was looking."

The kids illuminated the wall with their flashlights and Eve moved to shine her light at the angle from down the tunnel as Tim had done when he first spotted something. "There it is," Tim said as he quickly moved to a spot on the wall that was just behind him. "Thanks, Eve, I must have gone too far." Tim focused his light on a rough area of the stacked stone wall and in between the short sides where two stones met. "It feels like metal," he said as he pried at the wall with his index finger and thumb.

"Do you think you can get it out?" Riley asked as she peered from behind Tim, shining her light on the spot.

"I think so," Tim said, "I'm going to work at it gently."

"Is it gold?" Finn asked.

"I don't think so, but there's a tiny line of gold on the outside edge. The rest of it is pretty dark," Tim said as he worked to get the metal out of the wall.

"I'm going to search along the ground in this area too, just in case," Finn said, and he began to crawl along the ground looking closely at the area nearest to the wall.

"It feels round, for sure," Tim said.

"Do you think it's a coin?" Riley asked.

Tim shook his head. "I think it's too thick to be a coin." He finally separated the object from the wall. "Got it!" He examined the object under his flashlight as Finn hopped up and joined Riley, Eve, and Tim. "I think it's a button," Tim said as he turned the object over, then over again.

"What's on the front?" Eve asked.

Tim looked closely, "It looks like an eagle with something in its talons." He rubbed at the button with his thumb. "I think it has a patina. The color has darkened and is uneven, probably from being down here for so long, but nothing's coming off.'"

Riley inspected the object. "There's a slice of gold on the side," she said. "I bet it's bronze. I'm guessing the gold side was facing out?" she asked Tim.

"Yeah, that's the only way I spotted it," Tim said as he looked the object over again. "It looks like there's a shield in the center of the button with a 'C' on it."

"For real?" Finn asked as he looked closer. "You're right! This could be a Confederate button. We should get it cleaned up and research what type of person would have worn it."

Riley thought about the button and where it was found. "It seems like it could have been on someone's arm, and it caught on the wall. Maybe as they were running?"

"Or," Finn offered, "maybe someone was pushed up against the wall, and the button got lodged in between the stones." He positioned himself so that his chest pressed up against the wall.

"Could be," Riley said as she imagined how the button got wedged into the wall. She loved making up stories of what might have been. She felt giddy. "Maybe someone had this," she held up the cipher disk, "and they were being chased, and then got pushed up against the wall and searched for what they were carrying."

Finn completed her story. "But, the person being chased had enough time to jam the cipher disk in the crevice between the wall and the floor back there," he pointed to the way they had come from, "before being caught here and slammed up against the wall to be searched."

The friends all got a good laugh out of this. Tim said,

"Is this what you two do in your free time? Make up stories about stuff like this."

Riley and Finn laughed. "Pretty much," Finn said. "You know, when we're not ghost hunting or saving dogs." Riley laughed at this, but immediately thought of Buster when Finn said that last part. The dog she couldn't seem to save, and here she was on a treasure hunt. Finn seemed to notice and quickly changed the subject. "This looks like a button from a Civil War uniform. We'll get a good look at it when we get above ground and do some research online."

Riley was ready to move on. "Eve, make a note of the number of steps, Tim, mark the wall where you found the button, and Finn, give Eve your compass direction. We should probably start heading back."

The four friends knew they were getting close to being back at Bulloch Hall when they spotted the door that they assumed went to Mimosa Hall. "Should we try it?" Eve asked, looking at Riley with her eyebrows raised.

"We could," Riley said.

"Or," Finn suggested, "we could go past the door to Bulloch Hall and see what lies beyond it."

"I vote for that," Tim said. "If you're pretty sure this door goes to Mimosa Hall, what are we going to do? Go in and walk around the old house? I don't need to get arrested for trespassing." This made all four of them laugh.

Riley said, "Tim's right. We're pretty sure that door leads

to Mimosa Hall, but we don't know where the tunnel goes in the opposite direction from Bulloch. So let's check it out."

"Cool!" Finn said, excited for more adventure. "Maybe we can find out if it connects to the tunnel that goes to the Public House?"

The kids passed the door to Bulloch Hall, and the trusty glow stick that lay on the ground just before the door and continued walking. As they continued walking, there was a noticeable turn in the tunnel. Finn looked at his compass. "We were heading southwest, but now we're heading southeast."

"Toward Barrington Hall?" Eve suggested.

"Yep," Finn agreed, "that totally makes sense. If that old man was right, that's where we should be heading, toward another of the founding family's homes."

"That guy knows his stuff, huh?" Tim asked.

"Yeah," Finn said, "He seems to be pretty accurate so far."

After a while of encountering nothing but stone walls and dirt floor, Riley said, "I re-started my pedometer at the Bulloch door, and we're at just under 3,500 steps." She looked at Finn. "Are we still heading southeast?"

Finn looked at his compass. "Yep."

"I think I see a door," Eve said as her light shined on the left wall ahead of them.

"And the tunnel keeps going," Finn said. "This is so cool."

Riley thought about where they were and where the tunnel might lead, then she thought about what they had experienced when they were in the tunnel on the other side of the square. "Do you want to try this door?"

"No," Tim said, "let's note the number of steps and everything and keep going. If this leads to Barrington Hall, we might walk in on a tour."

Eve said, "If I'm going to map this properly, I'd kinda like to know where we are."

Tim eyed the length of the tunnel, drawn to what may lead ahead. "We can check it on the way back. If the old man is right, it totally makes sense for this to be the Barrington connection. Let's just go a little further to see what else we might find." He smiled hopefully at Eve. His eyes pleaded to continue down the tunnel.

"Okay," Eve said with a conciliatory smile, "but if we find another door, we have to check it out."

She made a note and Tim said, "It's a deal." He headed down the tunnel at a quick pace, scanning for more treasure.

As they continued walking, Riley lagged behind and was still searching the ground for any signs of a dog or treasure, but Finn seemed to sense something was wrong. "Every-thing okay?" he asked.

Riley slowed a bit to leave more space between them and Eve and Tim. "Yeah," she whispered, "I was just thinking about that awful feeling we got in the tunnel on the other side of the square."

Finn took in a deep breath then looked at Riley earnestly, "Do you want to keep going?"

Riley hesitated. "Yeah, let's go a little further and see if we find anything interesting, but if we get a weird feeling..."

"We turn around," Finn said finishing her thought.

"Hey guys," Eve called back to them. "We found something!"

Riley and Finn looked at each other, then down the tunnel where they could see the distant flashlights of their friends. "It's another door," Tim called back to them.

Riley and Finn jogged up to meet their friends. "Another door?" Finn said. "But, if we were correct that the doors led to the founders' homes, this one doesn't make sense."

"Right," Riley added. "The one past Bulloch should be for Barrington." She thought about the layout of the town above them. "There's nothing else this close to Bulloch that connects to the founders. Heck, we might be under Atlanta Street at this point."

"We have to check this one out," Tim said.

"Why not," Finn said. "It's intriguing that it's so close to Barrington, but not the door we think is Barrington."

"Or, this one leads to Barrington, and the one back there goes somewhere else," Riley suggested.

"Guys, we have to check it out so we can properly map this place," Eve said. "We can't just keep walking past all these doors."

"You're right," Riley agreed. "Let's see where it goes."

Tim said, "Let's just be quiet, in case it does lead into Barrington."

"Good idea," Riley said as she slipped her key necklace over her head and put the key in the iron lock. She turned the key hard, and there was a loud click. They all remained still and quiet just in case someone was on the other side of the door and heard that loud click too.

"You open it," Riley whispered to Finn as her heartbeat sped up.

Finn grabbed the iron knob and turned it clockwise. The metal made a scraping sound. He paused before pulling the door toward him. Like the door at Bulloch Hall, this one felt like it hadn't been opened in a long while, and it caught a little before pulling free from the jamb and Finn had to pull with some force. The four kids looked into the opening and saw another tunnel, like the one that led to Bulloch Hall. It had a ceiling that lowered and, hopefully, a hatch at the end. "You two stay here," Finn said to Eve and Tim. "Riley and I will go check it out. If there's someone on the other side, there's no sense in all four of us getting caught."

With that, Finn and Riley crawled to the end of this short, low tunnel and found a hatch door above them. Finn motioned to himself and then the hatch, gesturing that he was going to push up on it. Riley nodded and stayed quiet. Finn pushed up on the hatch, but it was too heavy and tough to budge. Riley looked at him and raised her eyebrows. Her headlamp illuminated his face and vice versa. Finn nodded. He needed her to help. The two friends stood back-to-back and pushed up on the hatch, and it gradually started to loosen a bit as dirt started to fall on them. They both squinted their eyes to keep the dirt out. They pushed a little harder and were shocked at what they saw - sunlight!

Riley and Finn pushed on the hatch door with even more force and peered through a three-inch crack. "We're outside somewhere," Riley said quietly as dead, brown magnolia leaves dropped into the tunnel.

"I think I'm looking at a stone wall," Finn said to Riley who was on the other side of the hatch door.

"I think we might be on the grounds of Barrington Hall," Riley said. "Look out this side."

"Are you sure?" Finn asked as he held his hands up on the hatch door and turned around, moving over to Riley's side of the tunnel.

"I think so," Riley said. "It looks like we're under a magnolia tree, but there's definitely a big, old, white house right there."

"You're right," Finn said. "This is so awesome! I have an idea. I'll get something to mark this, and we'll search above ground, so we don't get caught popping out of a hatch."

"Good idea," Riley said, smiling. "It's such a nice day that people are going to be out and about."

"Can you hold this for a sec?" Finn asked motioning to the hatch door.

"Yeah," Riley said.

Finn slipped off his backpack and rummaged around. "I think I still have some of that bright surveyor's ribbon we used near the caves." Riley could hear him digging at the bottom of his bag. "Yep, here's a piece," he said as he pulled out a ten-inch long piece of pink plastic ribbon. He braced the hatch with his right hand and positioned the ribbon so it was three-quarters of the way out of the hatch. "Let's close it carefully, and I'll hang onto the ribbon," he said. "Hopefully when it's closed, we can spot the ribbon above ground."

The two friends carefully closed the hatch so the ribbon stuck in the opening. Riley looked at Finn and could see excitement on his face; his eyes danced with the light from their headlamps, and a smile played on his mouth. "Looks like we have some above-ground exploring to do," Riley said.

"Yep," Finn said. "And depending on where this hatch is, this could mean we can explore the tunnels any time we want. We won't have to worry about making your mom suspicious with constant ghost hunting in the cellar of Bulloch Hall."

Riley smiled at her best friend. "Yes, this will make it much easier. Let's go tell Eve and Tim!"

With that, the two friends crawled back to the main tunnel with Riley leading the way to let their friends know they had a new way to explore.

CHAPTER THIRTY-THREE

Searching the Magnolias

Excited about the hatch they had found that led to the grounds of Barrington Hall, Riley, Finn, Eve, and Tim couldn't stop talking about the tunnels and how they might have been used. They quickly made their way back to the hatch at Bulloch Hall, closed everything up tightly, and said their goodbyes to Riley's mom. The friends wanted to get to the grounds of nearby Barrington Hall right away to figure out the location of the hatch door. As soon as they got off the porch at Bulloch Hall, Finn pulled what he thought was a Confederate cipher disk out of his pocket. He stopped in his tracks as he admired their find in the bright sunlight. "You guys! This is totally a Confederate Cipher disk. I'm sure of it!"

"That's so cool," Riley said as Finn handed it to her so she could admire her find.

Finn looked at Riley. "You found it, you should keep it."

Riley smiled. "Thanks, but why don't you hang on to it and research it first. I need to find out why Baby Girl showed me these tunnels, and more importantly, if they can help me find Buster." While her friends focused on treasure, Riley focused on Buster and the clue that Baby Girl had given her.

Finn smiled sympathetically. "I understand." He accepted the disk from Riley and tucked it safely back into his pocket.

Tim inspected the button that he found wedged into the wall. "I think you're right, Finn. This looks like a Confederate button of some sort. I quickly searched online, and it looks like this." Tim held up his phone and showed them a shiny button that looked similar to what they had. "I think the C stands for cavalry."

"This is so exciting," Eve said. "My dad and Evan would love to see this stuff. They're such history buffs, especially Civil War history. They may be able to give us some more info."

Finn looked at Eve. "We would have to agree not to tell them where we found it." He looked at all of his friends. "We need to be careful. If we start telling people where we found this stuff, we may not be able to access the tunnels anymore, and we're not even supposed to know about them ourselves."

Riley was thinking. "Yeah, if the disk is as big a find as Finn says, it could make news. Then other treasure hunters would want to go looking and surely the city would lock them up tight. Look what happened when we got caught in the hatch at Smith Plantation. It got a brand-new padlock right away."

Tim said, "How about we show Evan pictures of what we found and see what he says about them?"

Finn nodded. "I like that idea. We don't have to say we found them. We could just ask about them."

"Is that okay, Eve?" Riley asked.

Eve nodded. "Yeah, you're both right. We can't let anyone know what we found or where we found it."

"Cool," Finn said. "Let's head over to Barrington to see where that hatch is!"

Barrington Hall stood on a hill overlooking the town square, and a stacked stone wall encircled the property along Atlanta Street and the equally busy, Marietta Highway. The kids had to go to that intersection to catch a light to cross Marietta Highway. Once across the street, they climbed steep cement steps to the sprawling grounds of the beautiful antebellum home.

"It's so pretty," Eve said. "It looks straight out of *Gone with the Wind*."

As the kids walked along the gravel path, Riley said, "It does. We're so lucky these old homes are still standing. They are part of what makes Roswell so special."

"There's just so much cool history in Roswell," Finn said as he surveyed the area. "So, I saw a stacked stone wall like this," he said as he gestured to his left."

"And I definitely saw a magnolia tree," Riley said.

Tim looked around the expansive grounds. "It looks like the wall only goes along the front side of the property, and this side," he said as he gestured to the same wall Finn had. "There aren't trees lining the front wall, so we should probably check out the side wall first."

"I agree," Finn said. "And we saw the side and back

corner of the house, I think." He looked at Riley for confirmation.

Riley nodded. "Yep, I'm pretty sure it was the side and back of the house that we saw."

"Then let's head down this pathway and look for magnolia trees," Eve said motioning to the path that appeared to lead to the side garden, versus the one that led right to the front steps of the home.

When the kids got to the spot where trees began to line the wall, Eve got excited. "There's a magnolia!" She hurried over to the tree, and her friends followed.

As they walked through the layer of dead leaves surrounding the huge tree, Finn said, "I think it's good that we look, but we're still along the front corner of the house."

Riley agreed as she looked over at the large white house. "Yeah, we should look, but I'm pretty sure we were further back on the property."

After finding nothing, the kids walked back out from under the thick canopy of trees and continued along the tree line. "The magnolias have stopped, and these are some kind of holly," Tim said.

The kids walked through the far end of the formal garden and Riley marveled at the live archway that formed a tunnel from one end of the garden to the other. She stopped to admire it. "That's so pretty," she said as she took out her phone and snapped a picture of the trellised vines that created the feel of a secret garden. She looked at her phone and said, "Gee, I should have taken a picture from the hatch."

Her friends laughed, and Finn said, "I should have too. I

guess that would have been too easy."

Opposite the trellis stood a pergola with a bench swing hanging from it. "Yet another type of hedge," Eve said, noting the tall evergreen trees that now lined the wall.

The kids continued to walk toward the back of the property and on the edge of the formal garden sat a bench. "Look!" Riley said. "Behind the bench there's a wall and a row of magnolias. This feels more like it."

The four friends moved past the bench and underneath the shade of the huge magnolias that lined the stone wall. "Now, this is like a secret garden," Tim said.

"Keep your eyes peeled for bright pink," Finn said. "The survey ribbon should stand out."

Riley looked back at the impressive home. "I think we need to go a bit further back, but let's definitely keep an eye out."

The kids walked slowly, looking for the bright pink ribbon. "So far," Tim said. "All I see are brown tones from all these old leaves."

"I know," Finn said as he looked up ahead, their footsteps making crunching sounds as they walked through decaying leaves. "But look, the magnolias end, and then it's those holly bushes again."

Riley looked at the house again. "We should be close." She could smell the sweet perfume of the white magnolias that were blooming on the trees as they walked amongst them. The large white flowers were bigger than her hands and so elegant.

"I sure hope we marked it well enough," Finn said,

doubting himself as they neared the end of the magnolias.

"Look!" Eve said as she hurried to a spot on the ground, squatting down and moving large magnolia leaves out of the way. She looked up at her friends with sparkling, amber eyes as she pinched a length of neon pink surveyor's ribbon. "I think we found it!"

Finn exhaled in relief and hurried to Eve's side. He smiled broadly. "Yep, this is it!" He looked at Tim. "Help me move all these leaves."

Finn and Tim started clearing the leaves away by hand, but the covering was so thick they decided to use their feet to move them more easily. Once the leaves were mostly cleared, Finn squatted low again. "Now we have to get through all of this." He scraped at dirt and decaying plant debris that was underneath all the leaves. "There's no telling when this was last used, so aside from the rain, I bet nothing has moved this dirt in a really long time."

"This is so exciting," Eve said. "I wonder what they used all of these tunnels for."

"Isn't it crazy to imagine?" Riley asked. "I mean, it's pretty cool."

After Finn and Tim cleared away a lot of the dirt and debris, they could make out the rectangular outline of the hatch door. "It's a good thing we found it underground," Finn said as he wiped the dirt from his hands. "When we pushed up on it, we made this part much easier on ourselves."

"Do you think there might be some kind of handle to get it open?" Eve asked.

Tim scraped at the dirt above the crease he had exposed

on the left edge of the hatch door. "You'd think it would be right around here," he said, working to clear away the dirt.

Riley thought about it. "If this thing is as old as we think it is, a pull or handle might not even be here anymore." Riley swung her small nylon backpack off her shoulders and pulled out a bottle of water, gently pouring it over the area where Tim had been working. "Look," she said, "it's pooling in this area. Maybe this is where the pull was?"

Finn shined his flashlight on the spot and gently swept around the area with his index finger. "I think they carved the wood so they could attach a ring to it. Let me see if I have something to work at the dirt in this spot." Now, Finn rummaged through his backpack and pulled out his multi-tool. He opened the slot for the small flathead screwdriver and gently worked at the groove he felt in the wood. "Yep, I think they carved this so a ring would fit under this piece right here." He ran his finger across a straight line of wood that had indentations on either side of it. "If I can get enough dirt out, we can put some string or something through it so we can pull up on it."

"Couldn't we just pry the hatch open?" Eve asked.

Finn didn't look up as he continued to work. "The wood is too thick. We'd need to get a much larger tool, like a crowbar, and I don't have one of those in my bag."

The kids laughed and Tim said, "It's too bad we don't have that tool from the kitchen at Bulloch Hall."

Finn agreed as he kept working. "I know, right?"

"So, we need string or rope, right?" Riley asked.

Finn nodded, still gently working at the dirt. Without

looking up, he said, "Luckily, Eve and I wear sneakers with shoelaces. We should be able to use a shoelace to get it open." He looked up at Riley and smiled.

"So, sue me," she looked at Tim, "and my doppelganger for being lazy and wearing slip-on sneakers," Riley said, laughing and referring to when Tim was mistaken for her namely because of the slip-on checkerboard sneakers they both wore.

Tim smiled too. "At least I'm not wearing flip flops."

Finn continued to work and Eve looked at Riley and said, "He almost wore flip flops today."

"Okay," Finn said, "I think I have enough space to get a shoelace through." He sat back and untied his sneaker and pulled the lace free from the shoe. He worked the tip of his pinky finger into the small hole he had made then worked the end of the shoelace through. Once through, he pulled the lace even and tied a strong knot at the top. He stood and said to Tim, "Let's pull on three." Tim grabbed a hold of the shoelace. "One, two, three..." The boys pulled on the string, and the hatch door opened just enough for Finn to stick his toe in the opening. Riley, Eve, and Tim squatted and pried open the door all the way.

As the kids peered into the hatch opening, Riley chuckled as she saw writing in the dirt below the hatch. "Finn was here." She smiled at Finn, "Really?"

Finn grinned. "I had to make sure we were opening the right hatch." He couldn't contain his excitement as his eyebrows arched high over his bright eyes, "Now we have a way to get into the tunnels any time!"

CHAPTER THIRTY-FOUR

Conferring with Evan

Riley and her friends were so excited about the exterior access to the tunnel system and the items they found that they talked about it all the way to Eve's house. Tim had a good idea to take close-up pictures of the items they had found on top of the wooden front porch of Barrington Hall so the background would be neutral. When they got to Eve's house, they waved to her dad who worked in his office off the front hallway, then headed straight back to the kitchen which was open to the family room where Evan played a video game.

"Hey, Ev," Eve called to her brother as she opened the refrigerator.

Evan didn't look back when he replied, "Hey!"

"So, we've got lemonade, sweet tea, and water," Eve said as she scanned the fridge.

This made Evan pause his game and look in their direction. "Oh, hey guys. I didn't realize you were all here."

"Hi," Riley said. "We were hanging out around the square, and thought we'd come back here for a snack."

"Plus," Tim said, "We wanted to pick your brain about Civil War stuff, if you have time."

"Cool," Evan said as he put the controller down and joined them in the kitchen. "Why are you guys interested in the Civil War over summer break?" He said with a smile as he grabbed various snacks out of the pantry and set them out on the small kitchen table for everyone.

The kids sat around the table, and Finn said, "You know Riley and I are really interested in history, and there's so much around here."

"Yeah," Riley offered, quick with her thinking. "My mom is volunteering as a docent at Bulloch Hall, and they've got some great memorabilia in a couple of the rooms. Plus, the welcome center has artifacts that were found around Roswell. It's really interesting to think about what might have happened around here."

"Yeah," Evan said as he filled a glass with lemonade, then situated his tall frame into a chair at the head of the table. "A lot did happen around here, and the Historical Society has all kinds of information on Roswell during the Civil War."

Tim said, "We have some pictures of artifacts that were recently found in Roswell and wondered if you knew much about them." He tapped at his phone and showed Evan the picture of the button.

Evan looked closely at the screen and zoomed in on the item. "It looks like a cavalry button from the Civil War. It needs to be cleaned up, but that's what it looks like to me." He handed the phone back to Tim.

Tim scrolled to the next picture, knowing this item was more notable than the button. "What about this?" He showed the screen to Evan whose eyes got as big as saucers.

"This was found in Roswell?" Evan asked, grabbing the phone more quickly this time.

"Yeah," Finn said, and he knew his hunch about what it was had been correct. "Pretty cool, huh?"

Evan looked at Finn. "Do you know what this is?"

Finn said, "I think it's a Confederate Cipher Disk."

Evan nodded. "Uh, yeah, and they are really rare." He looked at Tim, "Where was this found?"

"Not really sure," Tim said, "It's in a private collection." Finn felt the weight of the item in his pocket and felt bad that they weren't being one-hundred percent truthful, but he knew they couldn't be right now.

"But you're sure it was found in Roswell, not somewhere else?" Evan asked.

"Pretty sure," Tim said as he gave Finn a quick glance while Evan's eyes were glued to the screen.

"That's a big find," Evan said, looking up at them. "Not just because it's rare, but that would mean a spy was here in Roswell, and that's really notable."

Just then, the kids heard Detective Rycroft emerge from his office, and he was in a hurry. "Hey kids, Glenn just got a lead on a case we're working on, and I have to head out." He grimaced. "I'm afraid I might be late, and I know I won't be able to cook dinner."

Eve smiled sweetly at her dad. "It's okay, dad. Evan and I can fend for ourselves."

He walked over and gave Eve a kiss on her forehead. "I'm sorry, sweetheart. This could be a big break." He grabbed a granola bar off the table and put it in his pocket. "This might be my dinner," he said as he patted Evan on the shoulder.

"It's okay, dad. We've got it," Evan said with a genuine smile.

Riley felt bad for Detective Rycroft. It had to be hard being a single dad and having to run out on a case like this. She was glad to see that Evan and Eve were totally okay with it. "Sounds really important," Riley said to Evan as she heard the front door close behind his dad.

"Yeah, he's been working like a dog lately on some big case. I hope it's the break he's needs to crack it," Evan said.

"Me too," Eve said. "He's been so stressed lately."

"Do you have any idea what the case is about?" Finn asked.

"Nah," Evan said as he sat back in his chair and unconsciously flipped his hair out of his eyes. "My dad doesn't talk work with us. I think he sees too much stuff and wants to protect us from it."

"That's smart," Riley said. "I wouldn't want to know about the stuff he sees." She thought about the illegal puppy mill which had been hard enough and knew he saw worse.

Evan sat forward on his elbows. "If you guys can find out any more about this cipher disk, I'd be really interested to learn more. It could change history in Roswell!"

Riley and Finn made eye contact. This was indeed a big find, and confirmed they should keep this information to themselves for now.

CHAPTER THIRTY-FIVE

Humans Can Be So Cruel

The next day, Riley awoke with a start. She dreamed about Buster. In her dream, she wasn't sure where she was, but it was dark, and she felt like she was in a maze. She saw Buster, or a little dark shadow that looked like him, but then he was gone. She ran to catch up with him, frantically calling out his name. He appeared again, and just as she got closer, he disappeared again. This same scene kept playing out in her dreams until she heard what sounded like a lot of dogs barking incessantly. As her mind began to wake in the present, she could hear a dog barking outside, then another one answering its call. Riley was sweating and out of breath. That dream felt so real. She pushed herself up on her elbows and threw off the covers. Why couldn't she find Buster? There was no trace of him, alive or dead, and her mind started spinning with what-ifs. Riley squeezed her eyes tight and said a silent prayer for Buster's safe return. She didn't know what else to do.

After she ate breakfast, Riley asked Finn to meet her at her house so they could scour the area for any signs of Buster, just in case. When Finn arrived with Molly at his side, Riley told him, "I had a dream about Buster. I saw him, but I kept losing him in this dark maze. Then, before I woke up, I heard lots of dogs barking non-stop." She squatted to greet Molly and petted her around her neck and chest.

"That's crazy," Finn said. "I wonder what it means?"

Riley stood, closed the front door, and joined Finn on the porch, waving to Hawk who was doing yard work. "Do you think it means he's still alive?" Riley swallowed hard, willing her tears to stay put.

She could tell Finn didn't know what to say as he shifted his weight from one foot to another, then shrugged. "I don't know, Ri. He's been gone a long time."

"That's the thing," Riley said hopefully, "if he had been hit by a car, he would have turned up by now."

Finn looked her in the eyes. "You're thinking someone has him?"

Riley sighed with frustration. "I don't know." Her voice cracked as Molly looked at her and whined. "I just think if he had been hurt, or if someone found him loose, we would have found him by now. He can't have been on the run this whole time."

The kids and Molly walked down the porch steps, then down the walkway toward the driveway. Finn looked at her gravely. "That could mean that we might not ever find him, Ri."

Riley nodded as the dam broke, and tears spilled out of her eyes and down her cheeks. "I know," she sobbed trying to control her emotions as Molly leaned up against her leg and whined again, making Riley squat to pet her. She knew Molly sensed her emotions, and petting her sure did help.

She looked up at Finn and said, "But I can still try to find him. I can't just stop looking for him. Look at Baby Girl. She found her way back."

She could tell Finn was thinking as she buried her face in Molly's fur, giving the sweet dog kisses of appreciation. Finally, Finn said, "What if we just outright ask Baby Girl's mom if there's anything she can think of that might help us find Buster?" He paused, his eyes alight with recognition. "Why didn't I think of this sooner?"

"What?" Riley said as she stood in anticipation of hearing something, anything, that might help her find her beloved dog.

"Why don't we call all the other people whose dogs are missing and see what we can find out? Maybe we can find some sort of link?"

"That's a great idea," Riley said as she wiped tears off her cheeks. A smile finally appeared on her red face.

Finn said, "We could even go to The Downtown Pooch and ask them if they know any details before we call."

Riley nodded and said. "I'd hate to call someone only to find out that their dog had been hit by a car and injured...or worse."

"I know, but they will understand since your dog is missing too," Finn suggested.

Riley thought for a moment, then nodded. "You're right. If one of the other dog owners called me, I would be more than happy to help."

"Cool, let's go!" Finn said as they headed toward the street.

"I'm going to get Lennox," Riley said. "I asked Hawk if he could use the exercise, and he said we can take him with us."

"That's awesome," Finn said. "Molly will be so happy to see her friend."

"And," Riley said. "I figure maybe Molly and Lennox might catch a scent of Buster or something. You never know!" Riley knew she had to think positively. Thinking otherwise would do her no good.

Late that afternoon, the kids returned home and were exhausted. After dropping Lennox off, Riley and Finn said their goodbyes as they went home for dinner. When Riley got inside, she greeted her parents in the kitchen.

"Well, someone looks tired," her mom said.

Riley plopped onto a bar stool and faced her parents who were cooking dinner. "I'm exhausted. Finn and I were looking for Buster all day." Riley noticed her parents exchange pained glances.

"Any signs of him?" Her dad asked with raised eyebrows and hopeful eyes.

Riley shook her head. "No, but we did find out something interesting."

Her mom stopped chopping potatoes and said, "Oh yeah?"

Riley nodded. "We found out that all the missing dogs are still missing. No signs of them. Not hurt, not dead.

Nothing."

Riley's dad wore a questioning glance as he leaned toward her. "That *is* interesting."

"I think so too," Riley said. "You would think they would have turned up at some point, especially if they had been hit by a car or something."

Riley noticed creases between her dad's eyebrows as he said, "How did you find this out?"

"First, we went to The Downtown Pooch and asked Sam if she knew if any of the dogs had been found. She said the families have been checking with her to see if anyone had commented on the signs, or if any dogs had come in that looked similar. She said all of them are still missing. No sign of them at all."

"Do you think they've been stolen?" Her dad asked.

Riley nodded. "That's what we're thinking. We called each of the families and asked about their dogs. Two were stolen out of cars with the windows rolled down, and the rest disappeared from their fenced yards."

"Just like Buster," Riley's mom said with concern showing on her face, too.

Riley thought back to what she and Finn overheard detective Rycroft say to her parents. "Why would someone steal all these dogs?" Riley asked her parents.

Her dad inhaled sharply. "Sometimes, people will steal a dog just to get the reward money, but clearly that's not the case here because none of us has been contacted." Riley noticed him look at her mom uneasily before he said, "Other times, people will steal a dog, and then sell it to someone as if it's their own, just to make some fast money."

Riley felt her eyes burn, and a lump formed in her throat. She looked from her dad to her mom and managed to squeak out the word, "Really?" as tears welled in her eyes.

Her dad let out a big exhale and came around the kitchen island and hugged her in his arms. He smoothed his hand over her head and said, "I'm sorry, Roo. We may have to accept that we're not going to see Buster again."

With this, Riley lost it. She pushed back from her dad and wailed, "No, dad, I can't accept that! After all that Buster went through, and he was finally starting to relax and become comfortable. It's not fair! It's not right!"

Her dad hugged her tight, trying to calm her. "I'm so sorry, honey. We've done everything we know to do..."

As Riley sobbed into her dad's chest. Her mom came over and stroked her back, trying to help settle her. "Shhh," she said. "We won't stop looking or praying, Roo."

After a while, Riley's crying had subsided, and she looked at her parents; her face flushed beet red and covered in tears. "Please don't give up on him," she urged her parents.

Her mom squatted down to her level and said, "We won't, honey." She tucked Riley's hair behind her ear and looked at her with deep sympathy in her eyes. "We won't give up hope. Why don't you go upstairs and rinse off your face? Dinner will be ready in a little while." She gave Riley a kiss on her forehead.

Riley hugged her mom tightly and said, "Thanks for not giving up."

###

Riley was solemn at dinner that evening and was glad her parents had the news on in the family room so it could serve as a distraction, even though the news wasn't very pleasant. "Why are there so many bad people?" She asked to no one in particular after a story had just finished, and they cut to the weatherman.

Riley's mom smiled at her softly. "There's an old saying in news, 'If it bleeds, it leads,' and it seems to have gotten worse over the years. There are so many good people in this world, people like you, who just want to help others. Unfortunately, the news just doesn't cover those stories like they should."

Her dad set his silverware down and said, "I'm going to turn it off. We watch too much news, and you're right. It's too negative."

As her dad was just about to press the power button on the remote, he stopped. The red 'Breaking News' banner appeared on screen.

Riley heard the female anchor say, "We have breaking news from Pickens county tonight. According to the Pickens County sheriff's department, a dog fighting ring has been uncovered in a rural area. Reporters are headed to the scene, and we will have more details as this story develops."

Riley hopped up from the table and started toward the family room. "Oh my gosh!" she said just as her dad abruptly shut off the television. "Dad, wait! I want to see that." "No, sorry Roo," her dad said as he put his arm around her shoulder and guided her back to the kitchen. "Let's have a nice, quiet dinner, you can catch up on this story later."

"See, just like I said," Riley said as she walked to her seat at the table and plopped into her chair. "There are so many bad people out there. What kind of person do you have to be to want to fight an animal?"

"Yeah, that's so messed up," Hailey said.

Just as her mom was about to say something, the door-bell rang. "I wonder who that could be?" Riley's mom set her napkin on the table and got up to answer the door. "I hope it's not a salesperson. Why must they come by at dinner time?"

Riley continued to eat in silence, thinking about what kind of horrible people were fighting dogs and, what kind of shape those poor dogs must be in when she heard a voice she recognized. Why is Finn's mom at the door? she thought to herself as she hopped up and walked toward the foyer.

CHAPTER THIRTY-SIX

With Bated Breath

Riley rounded the corner and saw Mrs. Murphy standing in the foyer talking to her mom. She heard her say, "Rescue groups are there, and they've found some of the missing dogs from Roswell."

"What?" Riley said as she hurried over to her mom and Mrs. Murphy. "Did they find Buster? Where did they find the missing Roswell dogs?"

Mrs. Murphy's expression was grave, and she looked at Riley's mom who nodded and said, "Come in, we may as well all hear this at the same time."

When they entered the kitchen, Mrs. Murphy noticed the dinner table. "Oh, I'm so sorry. I wasn't even thinking, and I've disturbed your dinner."

Riley's dad got up and greeted their friend and neighbor, his brow furrowed and concern reflected in his eyes. "Is everything okay?"

Mrs. Murphy shrugged. "Honestly, I'm not sure. I was just telling Priscilla that some of the missing Roswell dogs have been found at the dog fighting site in Pickens County."

Riley's heart sank and tears began to well in her eyes again. "Is Buster there?" Tears flowed freely as she knew there was a reason Finn's mom would come to their house in-person. She feared the worst.

Mrs. Murphy regarded her with sympathetic eyes, looking as if she could feel Riley's pain. "We don't know yet," she said. "Rhonda contacted me because Angels is involved in the rescue and she knows about Buster. I'm waiting to get information on the dogs they've found. If Buster is there, it should be pretty easy to identify him as there shouldn't be many Yorkies at a dog fighting operation." Her voice trailed off as if she didn't know what to say.

"Why would they steal dogs from Roswell for dog fighting?" Hailey asked.

Riley looked at Mrs. Murphy, and the look on her face told Riley that she didn't want to answer that question. Riley looked at her dad. "Dad, why would they do that?"

Her dad inhaled deeply and exhaled sharply. He looked into his daughters' eyes, and Riley could tell he didn't want to have to explain this. "Sometimes, dog fighters will use smaller or weaker dogs to entice a fighting dog to actually fight."

"You mean they will make them hurt a smaller or weaker dog?" Riley asked, unable to even fathom someone doing such a thing.

Mrs. Murphy answered. "Unfortunately, yes. If a dog doesn't want to fight, dog fighters will do all sorts of awful things to try to get them to become more aggressive."

"That's awful!" Hailey said, and Riley saw tears sliding down her sister's cheeks now.

Riley's mom hugged both of her daughters tightly. "Oh,

girls, I'm so sorry. Let's pray Buster isn't there...or if he is, that he's safe and unharmed."

Riley began to sob uncontrollably. All she could do was think of poor, sweet Buster who had already been through so much in his four short years and being tormented by another dog, all because some nasty human being wanted that dog to fight. Riley's mom guided her and her sister to the sofa and sat with them, trying to comfort them. Their dad and Mrs. Murphy joined them in the family room.

Riley's dad paced and ran his hand through his hair. "When will we know more?"

Mrs. Murphy said, "We should know more in the morning. There are rescue groups on the ground, and they will triage all the dogs and have them evaluated. Since they've found some of the missing Roswell dogs, their priority is to identify any dogs that may have been stolen to be used as bait dogs."

These last two words made Riley start. "Bait dogs?"

"I'm sorry," Mrs. Murphy said. "I've said too much."

"It's okay," Riley's dad said, offering a much-needed change in direction. "Are you in contact with the team on the scene?"

Mrs. Murphy nodded. "Yes. Both the rescue groups and Nick Rycroft know to contact me if Buster is found."

"Detective Rycroft?" Riley asked as she sat up in her seat.

"Yes," Mrs. Murphy replied. "He's been working on the case of the missing dogs and got a tip yesterday. He and his partner were the ones to alert the sheriff's department, and they've been on the scene since the start."

Riley stood up. "That's why he rushed out when we were at Eve's house! He said he got a lead and left in a hurry." Riley felt a tiny glimmer of hope. Detective Rycroft knew Buster and how much he meant to Riley. She said a silent prayer that Buster was okay and thanked God for putting Detective Rycroft on this case.

"I'm so sorry I interrupted your dinner," Mrs. Murphy said. "I just knew you would want to know, and as soon as I hear something, anything, I will call you." She gave Riley's dad a hug, and then came over to the sofa and hugged Hailey and her mom. Riley was still standing by the sofa, and Mrs. Murphy looked her right in the eyes and placed her hands on Riley's shoulders. "Riley, don't lose faith. If Buster is there, we will find him."

Riley smiled, unsure of how to feel. She hugged Mrs. Murphy tightly and said, "Thank you for coming here, and please let us know as soon as you hear something, no matter what time it is." Riley knew that 'finding him' could mean the worst, but she had to put that out of her head as best as she could.

After Mrs. Murphy had come over, Riley lost her appetite, so her mom wrapped up her plate and put it in the oven to stay warm. Riley was grateful for this because around nine o'clock, her appetite appeared with a vengeance. She cried and talked with her parents, and they put the internet off-limits. No researching dog fighting and bait dogs because they knew it would make things worse. Instead, the family watched a movie together. Riley tried not to fret about Buster, but that was impossible. She thought about him the whole night. She attempted to go to sleep, but couldn't. Her mind turned with all the scenarios that could be imagined, most of them not pleasant. Riley went downstairs, turned on the TV, and worked on her laptop to keep her mind off of what had happened at that property in Pickens County. Sometimes getting lost in a new design made the time fly by. She must have nodded off because at some point in the wee hours of the morning, her mom nudged her shoulder, trying to wake her.

Riley squinted through tired eyes. "Mom? Dad?" She noticed Hailey too. "What's going on?" Then she remembered everything and was almost wide awake now. "Is it Buster? Did they find him?"

Riley's mom had tears in her eyes, and Riley feared the worst. Then her mom nodded and smiled. "Yes!" She burst out. "They found him. He's safe!" She held up her cell phone. "Mrs. Murphy just called."

"Hi Riley," Mrs. Murphy's voice sounded from the speaker on her mom's phone. "They've identified Buster, scanned his microchip, and he's safe!"

Riley jumped up as tears of joy streamed down her cheeks. Her dad stood next to her and put his arm around her. "He's gonna be okay?" Riley squeaked out amongst her tears.

"Yes," Mrs. Murphy said. "He's going to be just fine. He'll need some water and food and a good cleaning, but he

255

appears to be okay."

"When can we get him?" Riley asked anxiously.

"I'm helping with the transport, and they are allowing me to go first thing in the morning to get the missing Roswell dogs that are healthy enough to go home," Mrs. Murphy said. "I'll be in touch in the morning and let you know when I'm heading back to Roswell."

"Are the other missing dogs okay?" Riley asked.

"Most of them are," Mrs. Murphy said as some of the joy faded from her voice. "We got lucky because the perpetrators had an inkling that the police were onto them, so they had recently quieted down their operations. Otherwise, it could have been worse."

Riley exhaled and finally felt relief. She said a silent prayer of gratitude that her sweet Buster was going to be okay.

CHAPTER THIRTY-SEVEN

Grateful, Thankful, Blessed

Riley was surprised at how long she had slept and woke up the next morning around nine-thirty. When she saw the time, she bolted out of bed and raced downstairs where her parents made breakfast. Hailey was already eating at the kitchen table.

"Hey Roo!" her dad said with a smile, and she realized he looked happier than she had seen him in weeks too.

"Hey," she said as she looked around with concern. "Have you heard from Finn's mom? Is Buster going to be here soon?"

Riley's mom smiled sweetly. "Yes, they're going to be here in a little while. Plenty of time for you to eat and get dressed."

Riley couldn't wait to see Buster. Before she did anything else, she made sure Buster had fresh food and water waiting for him. "I think I'm going to wait to shower," Riley said to her mom who watched her with a smile. "Buster is probably going to need a bath."

"Good idea," her mom said as she headed to the nearby laundry room. "I'll grab a towel and his shampoo."

Riley sat down at the kitchen table, and her dad placed a

stack of French toast with a side of scrambled eggs in front of her. Riley's stomach growled as she saw this. "Thanks, dad." She smiled up at him, and he gave her a wink.

"Need anything else, Hailey?" her dad asked as he smiled at Hailey who was finishing her breakfast.

"No thanks, Dad. I'm good."

Riley felt like she was in a movie. Everyone in her family seemed lighter and happier. She had been so concerned about Buster and hadn't thought how it had affected her parents and sister. As she cut her French toast, she said, "I wonder who is behind all of this?"

"I was thinking about that too," Hailey said. "Imagine what kind of monster would do something like fight dogs."

Their dad who had seen his fair share of cases as a lawyer said, "Sometimes cases can surprise you. All kinds of people commit crimes."

"Yeah, but dog fighting?" Riley said. "That's pretty messed up. All dogs want to do is please you and love you, have a full belly and a safe place to live."

"That's what's so sad about it," her dad said. "For the most part, the dogs that they choose to fight are the most loyal. They only fight because their humans want them to. They are fighting to please their people."

"How do you know so much about it, dad?" Riley asked as she picked up a glass of orange juice.

Her dad pulled out a chair, sat down, and inhaled a deep breath. "Atlanta had a star quarterback who I followed throughout his college career. He was an incredible athlete and was really positioned to go far. Heck, he had already become successful in the pros, but he could never sort out his personal life. He got caught with drugs in the airport, then he was implicated in bank-rolling a dog fighting ring in his hometown. I guess you can say I went down the rabbit hole and learned a lot about dog fighting. More than I care to know, really."

"What happened to him?" Riley asked.

"He plead guilty to one felony charge, I think it was for moving dogs across state lines for fighting. He was sentenced to 23 months in jail," her dad replied.

"That's all?" Riley asked, her eyes wide with disbelief.

"Yeah, if they had a trial, it could have been much worse for him," her dad said. "He would have faced a lot more scrutiny and bad publicity. His co-defendants also pled guilty and stated that not only did he fund the operation, but he also…"

"Jack!" their mom hollered from the kitchen, stopping their dad from saying anymore.

"What? What did he do dad?" Riley pressed her dad for details.

Her mom walked over and placed a hand on Riley's shoulder. "Honey, sometimes you don't need all the details."

"We can just look it up online," Hailey said, clearly wanting to know more too.

Their parents exchanged pained glances and their dad sighed. "These people don't value animals' lives like we do." He hesitated to find the words. "Dog fighters will often… get rid of dogs that aren't performing well, or can't fight anymore. They found a lot of bodies on this guy's property."

Hailey gasped, "Oh my gosh!"

"That's horrible!" Riley said with disgust and could feel her blood pressure begin to rise.

"And they do it for money," their mom said with disbelief.

"We're so lucky that Buster is okay." Riley said as she realized now more than ever just how lucky Buster was to come out of that situation alive. She thought of Detective Rycroft and Glen and how hard Evan and Eve said their dad and his partner had been working on this case.

"It'll be interesting as we get more details," their dad said as he moved the conversation along then sipped his coffee. "If they are hosting fights on the property and gambling, that could get them in more trouble than the animal cruelty."

Riley shook her head. "When will people understand that we need stronger animal cruelty laws. If the punishment is greater, people might think twice about hurting animals."

"Yeah, and people who hurt animals usually end up hurting people, too," Hailey added.

As Riley ate, she and her family discussed all sorts of things related to dog fighting and who might have stolen their dog. Eventually, her mom had enough. "Okay, enough of this talk. It's making me sad and angry."

"Aren't you curious who stole Buster?" Hailey asked.

"Of course," their mom said. "But, let's not speculate any more. Once they are able to tell us more, they will."

"Your mom's right," their dad said. "As the investigation unfolds, we'll learn more. What's most important right now is that we get Buster home and make sure he's okay."

Riley nodded. "Even if he's okay physically, I worry about him mentally. He had come such a long way since he was rescued from that illegal puppy mill."

Her dad reached out and put his hand on her shoulder. "He's a tough little guy, and if he is emotionally scarred from this, we'll help him just like we did before."

Just then, the doorbell rang, and Riley jumped out of her seat. "Do you think that's them?" she asked as she ran toward the front door. Her family followed quickly behind.

Riley opened the front door, and there was Buster in Finn's arms. "Oh my gosh! Buster!" Riley squealed as Finn handed him to her. Riley cuddled him in her arms and kissed him all over his little head. She didn't even think about it, but she started seeing flashes of mud and dirt. She heard dogs barking all over, frantic. She felt hot and scared. Oh, she felt so scared. In the present, Riley could feel herself stumble and someone caught her.

"Roo, are you okay?" Her dad had one hand on her arm and another around her waist. His eyes filled with concern.

Riley came to. "Yeah, sorry. I just got light-headed," she fibbed, then caught Finn's eye.

"Let's get you inside," her mom said and offered to take Buster.

Riley handed Buster to her mom as her dad helped her inside. As her head cleared, she said, "It's okay, dad. I'm fine."

Her dad looked her in the eyes. Worry creased in his brow. "Are you sure, sweetheart?"

Riley smiled, "Promise. I think I was just so overwhelmed to see Buster." Gosh, she hated being untruthful, but she didn't know how to explain or control her "gift."

"He's so clean," her mom said, sounding surprised.

Finn's parents smiled as they walked through the foyer and into the family room. Mrs. Murphy said, "I just couldn't bring him home all dirty. After we left the other dogs off at the vet's office, we took Buster to one of those self-dog washing places and got him all spruced up for you."

"Kate, that's so sweet of you," Riley's mom said. "Have a seat." She motioned to the sofas in the family room. "Would you like some coffee?"

"That would be great," Mr. Murphy said. "It was an early morning."

Riley's mom set Buster down in the family room and before heading into the kitchen, said, "Even though the vets on-site examined him, I still want to take him to our vet." She observed Buster as she said this, as did everyone else in the room. "Just to be sure."

Riley watched Buster closely. She was so worried about how this might have affected him mentally. Buster sniffed the floor and went right under the coffee table, and Riley's heart sank a little. "He's scared," she said to no one in particular.

"That's understandable, Riley," Finn's mom said. "It may take him a few days to settle in. He was kept in a kennel run outside with several other dogs. It was hot and muddy, and we're not sure how much food or water they got. Sadly, it's normal if he's a little traumatized."

Riley sat on the floor and peeked under the table. "It's okay, buddy. You're safe now."

"Here," Hailey said as she joined Riley on the floor. "Offer him a treat."

Riley put a treat under the table in front of Buster, and he happily ate it. "Good boy," Riley said.

Hailey put a treat a little farther from Buster, and he got up and ate it, then laid back down, closer to them now. "Good boy!" the sisters said in unison. Hailey stood and went to the kitchen to get more treats.

Finn sat down next to Riley. "You okay?" he asked.

Riley smiled. "Yeah, thanks. He was so scared," she said so only Finn could hear.

"Do we have any idea who stole him?" Riley's mom asked Mrs. Murphy as she brought steaming mugs of coffee in for her guests.

She shook her head as she took a mug. "No. If the police know, they aren't saying anything."

"We'll probably hear more as the case develops," Riley's dad said. "For now, I'm just so grateful to have Buster back, and unharmed."

Riley was so grateful to have their sweet dog back too, but she worried about what kind of mental trauma he might have faced. Based on what he showed her, he was terrified, and that broke her heart.

CHAPTER THIRTY-EIGHT

From Ghost Hunters to Treasure Hunters

By the next weekend, Buster was doing a lot better. He had become somewhat of a "Velcro dog" and always wanted to be near Riley; he had to be touching her. If she wasn't around, he had to be near someone else in the Carson household, and they were all okay with that. While the case was still on-going, there wasn't much that Detective Rycroft could tell them, except that it was someone on their landscaping crew who had stolen Buster, and the other dogs that had been stolen in Roswell. Riley had Finn, Eve, and Tim over to see Buster, and they discussed the case in the basement.

"I can't believe it was your landscaper who stole Buster!" Tim said.

"I know," Riley said as she stroked Buster's back. "I remember seeing the landscaping truck that day. And no one would have suspected a landscaper going into people's yards and stealing their dogs."

"Exactly," Finn said. "He had opportunity, and surely the motive was money. He was probably being paid to steal dogs."

"You don't think he was running the dog fighting ring?" Eve asked.

"I mean, I don't know, but I'm sure there are more people involved, especially since this seems like a large operation. On the news they said there could be over seventy dogs found at the property." Finn said.

Riley shook her head. "It's just awful. I don't understand how people can do such a thing."

Tim agreed. "I think those people are just plain evil. There's no other explanation for it. I mean, who could watch something like that?"

"I know," Eve said. "My dad was pretty upset about it and is putting in a lot of hours working closely with the sheriff's department, giving them all the information he has."

Riley looked at Eve. "So you have no clue how your dad figured this all out?"

"Nope, you know my dad." Eve said.

Her friends finished the famous line from her dad in unison. "We can't comment on an on-going investigation." Then, they all laughed.

Riley said, "It's okay. I don't want your dad discussing anything. I don't want anything to jeopardize this case. I want them to arrest every single person who was involved."

"Think about those poor dogs that didn't make it," Tim said. "And the ones that were badly injured."

Riley shuddered. "I know. It makes me so mad and sad. We're so lucky Buster wasn't hurt." She scratched him behind his ears as she said this, then looked at Eve. "I know we've already thanked your dad and Glen, but please make sure they know how grateful we are. This could have ended so much worse."

Eve smiled sweetly. "I will, but you know my dad knows how appreciative you are."

Riley smiled and said, "I have a thank you gift in the works." She grabbed her laptop off the coffee table and opened it up. She clicked to open an image and turned the laptop so her friends could see. "I designed this the night we found out about the dog fighting ring. I couldn't sleep and I was thinking about all the awesome people who were out there working late into the night to help the dogs."

On Riley's screen was a design that said, "Rescuing Dogs is My Superpower."

"I love it!" Finn said. "I know my mom will too."

Riley smiled brightly. "Thanks! I want to make t-shirts for your mom, Eve's dad, and Glen."

Eve was smiling too. "I think my dad and Glen will love it."

"Now we just have to wait and see what they uncover," Finn said. "In the meantime, we have something else to figure out."

That famous twinkle was back in Finn's eyes. "What's that?" Riley asked.

Finn reached into his pocket and pulled out a round metal object. "I cleaned this up. It's the Confederate Cipher Disk!"

Riley held out her hand. "Let me see." Finn placed the round metal object in the palm of her hand. "Wow! It's so clean. Look at all the detail!"

"Isn't it cool?" Finn asked proudly.

"While we wait for news of the investigation, we can look for more artifacts," Tim said.

"I've already asked for money for a metal detector for my birthday," Finn said, his excitement for what treasure they may find evident in his voice. "And, I'm going to start mowing lawns to earn money."

Riley handed the disk back to Finn. "Do you really think this means a spy was in Roswell during the war?"

Finn said, "If not a spy, then someone who would have been receiving messages."

"It definitely would have belonged to someone important," Tim said.

"That's so cool," Eve said.

"Don't forget," Riley said. "The cipher we found from Mr. Powell said that the tunnels were used to hide treasure."

"I'm *definitely* getting a metal detector," Finn said unable to contain his excitement.

"We need to research Jefferson Davis' treasure more, too," Riley said. "Maybe it really did end up coming through Roswell." Riley was so excited. She had Buster back and she and her friends were about to start treasure hunting in their hometown!

A NOTE ABOUT JEFFERSON DAVIS' TREASURE

Jefferson Davis was the President of the Confederate States and he fled Richmond, Virginia in April of 1865 as Union troops were closing in at the end of the Civil War. Davis and the rest of the Confederate government fled south, supposedly taking with them the treasury of the Confederacy: large sums of gold, silver, and other coins. While there is no record of Jefferson Davis going to Roswell (maybe some of the treasure made it there!), he was captured in Irwinville, Georgia, but had very little money on him. To this day, no one knows what happened to the Confederate treasure and treasure hunters all around the United States have been searching for it for all these years.

Will Riley, Finn, Eve, and Tim find the treasure?

Stay tuned for book 4 in the Riley Carson Series!

***

A SPECIAL CLUE JUST FOR YOU!

Flip the pages toward the very end,
Next to the page where you'll see me and
my best friends.
You'll find a clue leading to another book.
If you've read about the caves, you'll know
just where to look!

I HOPE YOU ENJOYED BOOK #3!

Riley Carson will return in book #4, so stay tuned for more dogs, adventure...and treasure!

If you want to stay up to date with everything Riley Carson, head over to **www.RileyCarsonSeries.com** to sign up for my mailing list and get the free e-book, *Introducing Riley Carson*! Just make sure to get your parent or guardian's permission. In the free prequel, we meet Riley, her first dog Sammy, and, it marks the first appearance of Hawk!

You can also find free resources and links to buy Riley's designs on t-shirts, stickers, and more!

Don't forget, there's a special clue toward the end of this book. Keep reading...!

AUTHOR NOTES

Roswell, Georgia is a real town north of Atlanta. If there are any tunnels underneath the city, they are a mystery to me! The tunnels are my creation, but I think it would be cool if they really did exist. In fact, while writing this book, I was telling a real estate agent I worked with about the story and he told me that he spoke with a long-time resident of Roswell who said there were tunnels underneath the city. How cool is that?! The historic homes mentioned in the book are real and you can go tour them. It's a great way to learn about the history of the city and what life was like before and during the Civil War. When choosing a location for the kids to enter the tunnels, I scouted the historic homes and thought the basement of Bulloch Hall would be perfect! The building is as described in the book, however, I've never gone past the picket fence barricade into the root cellar to see if there is any sort of tunnel hatch! ;)

The Downtown Pooch is a real business on Canton Street in Roswell and that's where we do all our shopping for Finlay and Riley! The owner, Sam, always offers me a space on her lawn for book signings and I've gotten to meet so many readers and wonderful dogs with their humans at The Pooch! If you're in Roswell, you must stop by and say hello!

General Sherman came through Roswell and many think that the historic homes were spared because the families put Masonic symbols on the outside of the homes knowing that Sherman himself was a Mason. Union soldiers did stay in the homes when they occupied Roswell and many artifacts from the Civil War era have been found all over Roswell. You can see many of these at the Roswell Visitors Center. The Confederate cipher disk that I wrote into the story would be an extremely valuable artifact if found. From my research, only 3 are known to exist!

Dog fighting is a felony offense in all 50 states and is a felony under federal law too. Unfortunately, this doesn't stop it from happening and many of these operations fly under the radar. The story about the Atlanta football quarterback is true. Sadly, dog fighting is a reality in the United States and the world. I will never understand why people do this and how they can watch animals hurt each other. While low-level dog fighters will steal dogs to use as bait dogs, in general, larger operations (as described in this story) tend not to do that. Upon speaking with Detective Michael Duffey, Animal Cruelty Investigator, I learned that large fighting operations wouldn't usually pit one of their dogs against a submissive pet that was stolen, rather, they would use one of their own dogs that doesn't show a desire to fight. I hate even writing about this here because it's so troubling, so if you want to learn more, there are plenty of resources online including:

https://www.humanesociety.org/resources/
dogfighting-fact-sheet
https://www.aspca.org/news/
what-dog-fighting-and-what-can-you-do-stop-it

If you do decide to research this, just guard your heart. It's hard to read about what happens to dogs that are forced to fight. I know more than I care to, myself.

ACKNOWLEDGMENTS

As with everything, I thank God for the blessings He gives me, and writing these stories is indeed a blessing. My dear Michael, Finlay, and Riley...my everything, you inspire me and make life fun! My parents for your continued support and love. To my readers, thank you for reading my books and telling others about them, these books are nothing without you and I write them with love for you. Every writer needs a great group of beta readers, those who volunteer to read as I write so I can make my books the best they can be. Thank you to Catherine Campbell and Joy Southerland—the first readers to read this book! You read each version with enthusiasm and without delay, you don't know what a huge help that is to me! To Riley's Readers, my Advance Reader Team: Catherine, Joy, Sara, Daisy, Denise, Barbara, Mom, and Dad. Thank you SO much for reading the proof copy, providing feedback, and spotting those typos! You don't know how much this helps me and I am so grateful for your time, help, and support! My editor, Amanda Schuyler, thank you for helping me see what needed to go and how to shape this novel while staying true to my message. To Sam at The Downtown Pooch, thank you for your support and always having a space for me on your front lawn! Detective Michael Duffey, thank you for your insight on dog fighting and all your work to put an end to it.

A heartfelt thank you to all the people who work tirelessly for animals. You inspire me daily and I hope we can change the world for animals together, using the talents we have.

A special clue just for you!

59-5-3
85-17-4
27-26-4
183-8-11-12

Use this code for an exclusive surprise - just for those who would make great spies!

Enter the code here:
www.RileyCarsonSeries.com/code-breaker

ABOUT THE AUTHOR

Michael Duisenberg

Megan Wargula is a self-proclaimed "dog nerd" - the kind of person who knows the dogs in her neighborhood better than their humans! A native of Atlanta, Georgia, Megan has always loved animals and has made it her mission to make the world a better place for dogs through her writing. In addition to the Riley Carson Series, Megan designs t-shirts, accessories, and gifts for dog lovers under her brand, Hound and Thistle. In 2020, Megan and her husband, Michael, started a podcast/YouTube show called Dog Nerd Show where they talk all things dog! The inspiration for all of this are their dogs, Finlay and Riley (pictured above). Luckily for Megan, she gets to work from home and has the best little furry co-workers in the world! Megan is a fan of history and the paranormal which is part of the reason she loves the town of Roswell, Georgia so much. Many of the places in the books are real, so plan your visit!

Made in the USA
Columbia, SC
23 May 2022

60632354R00174